Young Gucci:

Love at First Swipe

Young Gucci:

Love at First Swipe

Niyah Moore

www.urbanbooks.net

Urban Books, LLC
300 Farmingdale Road, N.Y.-Route 109
Farmingdale, NY 11735

Young Gucci: Love at First Swipe
Copyright © 2020 Niyah Moore

ISBN 13: 978-1-64556-003-6
ISBN 10: 1-64556-003-1

First Trade Paperback Printing February 2020
Printed in the United States of America

10 9 8 7 6 5 4 3 2 1

Distributed by Kensington Publishing Corp.
Submit Orders to:
Customer Service
400 Hahn Road
Westminster, MD 21157-4627
Phone: 1-800-733-3000
Fax: 1-800-659-2436

Young Gucci:

Love at First Swipe

by

Niyah Moore

Chapter 1

Soraya

A single minute had passed since I last checked my iPhone, which seemed like an hour ago. It was 8:45 p.m. on a Friday, and I couldn't believe that I was sitting at home. This was the third Friday in a row with zero plans. I couldn't remember the last time my best friend and I got dressed and headed to our favorite seafood restaurant, the Water Grill. We would eat, drink, and gossip. Then afterward, we would go to any jumping nightclub and dance the night away, downing Patrón shots. We wouldn't get in until 4:00 a.m. the next day. Now that was what I called an exciting Friday night.

I was sitting at the kitchen table with my laptop, legs neatly tucked under me. My hair was braided to the side, draping over my left shoulder. Bored out of my mind, I scrolled through Snapchat stories. It would've been nice if I could've been getting ready for a date or something, but my love life had officially dried up like pieces of juicy mango placed in a dehydrator.

The TV was on in the living room, though I was only half watching it. A Single Ready to Mingle commercial came on, and it had me looking up from my laptop. I'd seen the commercial many times before, and each time it made me wonder if the people were paid actors, because it seemed so scripted. Yet I was intrigued by the scripted outcomes.

Can people really find love online? I asked myself. I had a few men get at me through Instagram DM and Facebook Messenger, but I never responded because social media platforms weren't for dating. At least for me, they weren't.

Where did I go wrong?

I had one true love once. His name was Jacoury, and we broke up the day he got arrested. He had to do some time, and I wasn't the type to do time with him. I dated here and there, but none of those situations materialized into anything worth mentioning. I wanted a commitment. I didn't do "me, he, and she." Just he and I. I wanted someone to love me the way that I loved him. What was the point of doing things for a man as if we were in a committed relationship when he wasn't trying to be anything more than a fuck buddy?

Where were the real men who wanted to court and weren't afraid to say they were looking for love too? Seemed like I wasn't going to find him in a grocery store, bank, club, or jogging in the park. Black love was trending on social media, surprise proposals, and weddings were all up and down my timeline daily. I was feeling left out, and getting married was looking more like a dream that would never ever happen for me. I was starting to lose hope. As my dirty thirties were approaching in two more years, what would it hurt to try the website out?

I typed www.singlereadytomingle.com into my search bar and cruised around the site to see if it would be hard to create a profile. It seemed like there were some promising prospects. The website stated it was free for women to sign up, so I shrugged and created a profile. I posted a couple of pictures since the site recommended to post more than one for better results. As soon as my profile was ready to go, I took a deep breath and hoped for the best.

My roommate, Kaeja, came out of her bedroom and walked past me into the kitchen. Not only was she my roommate, but she was my best friend and had been since we were freshmen in high school. I loved Kaeja's natural kinky, curly hair that looked like tiny, perfect spirals. Her dark skin looked like creamy chocolate milk, and her dimples were deep in each check even when she wasn't smiling.

"What you doing? Designing clothes?" she asked as she took a small bag of green apples from the refrigerator and placed them on the counter.

"I'm creating a profile on Single Ready to Mingle," I replied reluctantly. I felt a little embarrassed because I didn't want to sound like I was desperate.

"What?" Kaeja asked and then laughed.

"Don't laugh. I'm trying to see something."

"Girl, trying to see what?"

"I want to see if I can—"

"Can what? Find you a man up on there?" she interrupted.

I didn't respond as I bit my lower lip.

"Oh, wow."

"Wait, Kae. Listen to this." I read some guy's headline to myself and then aloud: "'Looking for Mrs. Right. Is that you?'"

"Is that his hook?" Kaeja scowled. "I wonder how many women responded to that lame-ass line."

"His profile name is Mandingo_69." I paused before laughing at how ridiculous that sounded.

Kaeja rolled her eyes. "Mandingo_69? Girl, delete your profile 'cause it ain't gonna work."

"No," I whined. "Not yet. I just got started. I only clicked on his profile because baby was cute, but how thirsty can this dude be with a profile name like that? He wants everyone to know he got a big dick and it probably ain't even big! And 69! He's making it known that he wants some head, but he's also saying that he gives head."

"Raya, it's a fuckin' thirst trap is what it is!" Kaeja shook her head, and her wild, curly hair shook with her. "I doubt you will find anyone who will be honest about who they really are, and you may end up in a dangerous situation if you meet up with any of them." Kaeja cut an apple into slices on a wooden cutting board. "He ain't looking for Mrs. Right. Maybe Mrs. Right Now. I don't even know why you're wasting your time. What made you want to create a profile anyway?"

"I read all these testimonials, and the commercials are interesting. I want what Remy and Pap have! I want hashtag black love! To be honest, I wouldn't mind having what you have with your boo."

Kae smirked as she wagged her pointer finger. "You gotta be careful what you wish for. Fuck around on the internet and find you a prison boo. You not holding nobody down, hence the reason why you're not with Jacoury anymore. Pap held Remy down when she did time, might I add. That's why they have black love."

"I am not fit to be nobody's prison wife!"

She nodded. "And that's why you need to stop while you're ahead. But um, speaking of Jacoury, you know he's fresh out, right?"

I took a deep breath and exhaled. I saw on Facebook that he was home. He had been for a few weeks. After doing five years in Salinas Valley State Prison, he was finally free, and I was trying my best to not notice. I thought about sending him a message on Facebook, but at the same time, I was in my feelings. Why hadn't he called me? My number hadn't changed.

Every time I thought about Jacoury, I couldn't help but reminisce on our good times. He had the most beautiful brown skin and chestnut brown eyes. Flashbacks of what used to be were something that never left no matter how hard I tried to push them to the furthest part of my brain. Suddenly, I imagined my hands rubbing the waves of his fade as he was nestled between my legs licking my clit like he could never get enough. I managed life for five years without him.

I shook off the memories with a shudder and replied, "I haven't spoken to him since he's been home. What I look like hitting him up now after I abandoned him? His words, not mine."

"Well, first of all, you can stop denying that you still love him. I've always said y'all have too much history to throw away. You two were together from the ninth grade until our third year in college. You act like he did twenty years. He only did five."

"I will always have love for Jacoury, but I can't go there. I told him that if he loved the streets more than he loved me, then I was done. He chose and ruined what could've been a bright future. Besides, I want something new and exciting."

"All right, but I'm issuing you my warning right now with this online dating shit. Don't bring no crazy-ass, deranged killers up in here, okay?"

"You think some killers up on here looking for love?" I joked.

"I'm dead ass, Raya. Might be some rapists looking for their next victim. You gotta be careful."

"You watch way too much *First 48*."

"You don't watch it enough. Those are true stories, Raya. Make sure to inspect all pictures. If a nigga only got one pic, he might not be who he said he is, so next. If he got hella pics of him out drinking, he's an alcoholic, next. If he got too many cropped pics, that mean he got a bitch, next."

"No worries. I got this."

I clicked on the filter button to reveal Los Angeles men only and scrolled through a few more profiles in the "Do You Want to Meet Me" section of the page. I clicked no on the profiles as fast as they came.

I came to an abrupt stop when I saw this handsome face with these penetrating hazel eyes. His screen name was YoungGucci90. Damn, baby was fine with his caramel self. I clicked on his profile. His height was the first thing that jumped out at me. He was six foot three inches, and he lived right here in Los Angeles. I had a weakness for tall men.

"Oooooh, shit," I said while fanning myself. "Look! He is fiiiiiine as hell!"

"There you go, looking at his physical appearance," she replied without looking at my computer screen. "First of all, what is his screen name?"

"YoungGucci90, and he apparently loves to wear Gucci."

"Gucci has made a huge comeback for the culture even with their blackface bullshit-ass apology. Nonetheless, it seems like everybody is wearing it again instead of boycotting it any further. What's he talking about on his profile?"

"Come look."

She took another bite of the apple slice and walked from the counter to me. I clicked on a picture of YoungGucci90 biting on his lower lip and looking at the camera all sexy like he was ready to devour anyone looking at him.

"You ain't lying! Girl, he's what I call too fuckin' fine. That might be a catfish situation for real. That can't be a real profile."

The *Catfish* show did scare the hell out of me. I didn't know how those people went years without seeing a person face-to-face but claimed they were in love. Those people were gullible and too desperate for me.

I took a more in-depth look at YoungGucci90's page. Chicks were posting how good it was to meet him and asking why he hadn't hit them back. Some of them were begging to see him again. He had to be a real person.

"This doesn't look like a catfish, Kaeja. Chicks posting and tagging him in stuff like he's real, so he must be."

"He looks like he hooks up hella much, and he looks like he's a little younger than we are. I don't think a man that fine is having a problem with getting ass," she griped as she stared harder at his pics. "Why he gotta be all up in the club? And there's a bunch of girls all over the place. Ah, hell nah! I would pass."

I frowned. "He looks like he knows how to have a good time to me. If he's over twenty-one, I don't have an issue with age. But I don't know. With these chicks begging like this, I'm curious. Let me read his profile some more."

She hummed as I continued to scroll through his page.

"He likes to work on cars. A man who isn't afraid to get his hands dirty, sweet. It looks like he has a hell of a car collection with a mixture of old schools and other foreign whips. Under his occupation, it says to ask him."

Kaeja went back to the counter to put her apple slices into a bowl. She sat down next to me, all the while shaking her head.

"What?" I asked. "Why are you looking at me like that?"

"I'm not saying anything, friend. If this is what you want to do, let me know when you want to meet him so I can be right there with you."

"Okay. You think I should send him a message?"

"Raya, you're my best friend in the whole entire world, and you're too fuckin' pretty to be all up on the internet looking for a man. You don't have low self-esteem, and there are plenty of real men out there. Soooo no, I don't think you should send him a message."

"Come on, Kae. Ain't none of the men I've been dating worth shit, and I'm tired of chilling alone. I want a boyfriend. Why is it so hard to have one?"

"You don't go out anymore. How can you meet someone when you're cooped up in the house?"

"True, but maybe my luck can change by meeting men I would never meet while out and about."

"Well, I don't think you're going to find the one on there. That's my honest opinion. Don't kill me."

"Let's see where this goes. Not everybody can have the perfect high school sweetheart," I reminded her. "If you weren't in a relationship, you would probably understand how I'm feeling right now."

"You and Jacoury had that high school sweetheart thing going!"

"Yeah, but he fucked it all up."

"You afraid you gonna hook back up with Jacoury, aren't you?" she asked with a weird smile forming. "I get it. You want to be unavailable because he's home now."

"No, Kaeja. Jacoury is an ex for a reason. It's time for me to see if I mesh with anyone else."

The front door opened and closed. Speaking of the love of Kaeja's life, Avian, her boyfriend, walked into our apartment as if he lived here. I was still mad that she had given him a key behind my back, but after she apologized, I had to act like I was okay with it.

Avian and Kaeja met at 15 years old, the same year Jacoury and I hooked up, but after thirteen years, she still didn't have a ring on her finger. All she ever talked about was marrying Avian, but Avian brushed over the subject as if marriage weren't an option. She pretended as if she weren't ready for the next step.

Avian was half Puerto Rican with long hair, which he kept in a ponytail. He wasn't as tall as I would like, but he was taller than Kaeja, and she didn't mind that he was under six feet tall.

"Hey, Avian," I said.

Avian walked into the kitchen with a duffle bag. He was dressed up in a nice pair of jeans and a button-up. As much as I didn't mind his company, being around them made me want to be in a relationship even more.

"Hey, Soraya," he said and then placed a kiss on Kaeja's lips. "Babe, why aren't you dressed?"

"I'm about to go get dressed right now," she replied.

She hadn't told me they were going anywhere. "Where y'all going?" I asked all nosy-like.

"We're going to the House of Blues. Chris Brown is supposed to be there," he replied.

"Should I wear a short black dress or the green one, Raya?"

"You stay wearing black every time you go out. Wear the green one. Hey, soooo why y'all didn't invite me?"

"I thought about asking you, but you always say you don't want to be the third wheel, and I didn't want to make you feel awkward. Plus Avian got the tickets."

"Thanks for lookin' out," I said to Avian sarcastically.

"My bad, Raya. For real, next time you can roll with us, and I can hook you up with a date," he said.

"Nah, I'm cool on ya hookups. The last one was cute but dry and boring. No, thanks." I picked up my laptop and headed to my bedroom. "You guys have fun."

As soon as I was in my bedroom, I closed the door. I couldn't stop staring at YoungGucci90's profile. Those eyes had me stuck. Even though Kaeja told me not to, I went ahead and sent him a message anyway. I typed:

Hello Young Gucci,

I came across your profile, and I wanted to introduce myself. My name is Soraya, and I'm 28 years old. I'm single, never been married, no kids, and I started my own clothing line called Paradise You. I'm five foot three, 145 pounds, and as you can see, I like to keep myself up. Why are you online looking for love?

   MissDesignDiva

I checked to see if he was online, but his profile said that he had already logged off an hour ago. I logged off, feeling a little disappointed. I turned on the TV and let out a long sigh. It was going to be yet another long and boring Friday night at home alone. I picked up my laptop again and checked the House of Blues website to see if there were any tickets left for this Chris Brown event. I crossed my fingers.

Chapter 2

Kaeja

"Babe, why is it taking you so long?" Avian complained. "You promised you would be ready before I got here."

"I'm so sorry, babe. I'm ready now," I said, making sure all my makeup was back in my makeup case in the bathroom before I walked out. I didn't know why he wanted to show up early. It wasn't as if we didn't already have VIP tickets. Plus Chris Brown wouldn't get on stage until the end of the night. We still had plenty of time.

I sashayed to the closet quickly for my heels so he wouldn't grow more impatient.

"I like that dress you're wearing," he complimented me. "I haven't seen you in that color before."

"Raya suggested I step outside my comfort zone and wear colors other than black. This one hugs me in all the right places, don't you think?"

He licked his lips slowly and gave a slight grin. "Hell yeah. You're blessed with all that ass. I'm one lucky bastard. You must want me to fight someone tonight, huh?"

I giggled as we walked out of my bedroom. "You won't have to do that, babe. Everybody knows I belong to you." I called out to Soraya, "See you later, Raya. We're gone."

"Bye. Have fun," she called back through her closed door.

We lived right in the heart of downtown Los Angeles, and it was perfect for us. We managed to find an apartment that was regulated by rent control, so the price did not increase every year. Soraya was self-employed, having launched her own clothing line, and I was a real estate agent who didn't make as much commission as I wanted. Rent control allowed us to afford the rent in case one of us couldn't come up with it.

Avian had his own place overlooking Venice Beach. He worked for Universal Music Group in A&R, so he had all the plugs in town and significant hookups. We didn't have to wait in line for anything. There were plenty of industry award shows, after-parties, luncheons, and mixers to attend that kept us busy.

"Hopefully traffic won't be too bad tonight," he said.

"Baby, this is L.A. Traffic is always bad."

"True, true. That's why I wanted to leave earlier."

We walked down the stairs and got into his black BMW 7 Series. As soon as he started up the car, a hard-hitting trap beat bumped through the speakers. I snapped my fingers while he opened the sunroof. The palm trees standing tall underneath the night sky looked so lovely. I loved living in Los Angeles. There was no place like it. He turned up the music more. Nothing was sexier than riding with my man down the streets of downtown, listening to music on our way to an event.

Soraya crossed my mind, as did the look on her face when she saw that we were going out without her. I felt terrible that I hadn't invited her out with us. That night was the first time she'd ever expressed that she felt lonely. She hadn't had a real boyfriend since Jacoury, but I didn't understand why it was so hard to date. Soraya was one of the most beautiful women I knew. Her honey brown skin glowed, and when she smiled, the whole room would light up. She was more than a best friend. She was the sister I never had, and I wanted what was best for her.

I didn't want to see her waste her time. Soraya belonged with Jacoury, but she was irrational. Although he was once an all-star high school basketball player and a damn good college ball player while we attended UCLA, he got caught with a gun and drugs, and he blew his chances of entering the NBA draft. He had to do time, and she had a zero-tolerance policy when it came to shit like that. She did not want to hold him down, and I didn't get it. He was a good man who made a wrong choice. He had to pay for his crime and had been judged already for it, so why was she so hard on him? I couldn't imagine how hard that was for him to lose the love of his life while behind bars.

He was released earlier than he expected, which was a good thing. Instead of getting back together, Soraya was looking for love online. It was crazy to me. Why wouldn't she rekindle her romance instead of trying to meet a stranger? Anyone could pretend to be anyone online. It was too scary.

Suddenly, Avian turned down the music. "What you over there thinking about?"

"We left Soraya home alone. I feel hella bad because I didn't even think to ask her if she wanted to come."

"I feel bad too. She did look sad. Listen, I'll make sure her name will be at the front door, so text and tell her to come up there if she wants to."

Avian turned the music back up before I could thank him. I smiled a little and pulled my phone from my clutch. I hit her with a text so she could get out of the house for the night.

Chapter 3

Soraya

The House of Blues event online was sold out. I blew air from my lips and sulked a little. Why hadn't Kae and Avian thought of me? Avian knew he could've gotten me a ticket, and that was what had me a little upset.

I gave up on trying to get out for the night, put on some shorts and a T-shirt, and got into bed. I pushed the guide on the remote to see if a good movie was on. I wound up settling on *B.A.P.S.* because I hadn't seen it in a few years.

I laughed at Halle Berry trying to dance on the sidewalk thinking she was about to kill an audition for a music video. After I laughed, I thought about how pathetic I was sitting at home watching this old-ass movie. Ugh, I hated being alone. I thought about scrolling through my phone to find someone to keep me company, but I quickly changed my mind. If I wanted to find someone new, I couldn't call up old work because I was bored. That was a lame idea.

My phone dinged, which surprised me. I picked it up, hoping it was someone worthwhile hitting me up to kick it. It was a text from Kaeja.

Kae: Avian left your name at the door, so come on.

I squealed, "Yessssss!" and sent a text back: Tell him I said thank you! See you soon!

I kicked off the covers and hopped out of that bed so fast. I unbraided my little raggedy braid quickly, walked to the bathroom in the hallway, took my wig off the wig holder, and plugged up my flat iron. I had to look cute, and I didn't have much time to do it. I already knew what I wanted to wear because I had been saving this dress I designed to wear for the next time I decided to head out. My little spirits perked right on up. Avian did not let me down and came through for me. I knew he could use his Hollywood status to get me up in there, and I was glad I didn't have to beg for it.

"Thank you, Jesus!" I proclaimed up to the ceiling.

I went back into my bedroom and took the azure blue dress out of my closet. I held it against me while looking in the mirror to make sure I still wanted to wear it. I nodded at myself. I was wearing this. I wanted a fine-ass man to see me in this shit and fall in love on sight. I didn't believe in love at first sight, but I felt so good, like magic was about to happen for me.

After turning on music through my speaker from the Bluetooth on my phone, I placed the dress on the bed. I quickly went back to the bathroom to take a shower. I was going to have to move quickly if I wanted to catch the show on time.

Lizzo's "Truth Hurts" was bumping as I drove toward the event. Sunset Boulevard in West Hollywood was backed up near the House of Blues. Go figure. Traffic was the worst in Los Angeles. I blew air from my lips while my car came to a stop. I couldn't help but look at my notifications while sitting to see if Mr. YoungGucci90 had logged on. I saw that he read my message but hadn't responded.

I sucked my teeth and wondered why he hadn't responded yet. I hoped he wasn't the type to read messages and not reply. I hated it when men did that. It was like damn, you could at least hit me back and say, "Hey, thank you, but I'm not interested in you," or something.

I tossed my phone over in the passenger seat, and the traffic started moving slowly. I had to tell myself not to take it hard if he didn't respond, but I really wished his cute ass would say something. Then I started thinking about it being a fake profile. That could've been the case. I hoped there would be some cute single men in there. Chris Brown usually brought a lot of single women out, so I expected the place to be filled with women. I only hoped there would be enough men.

"Relax, Raya. Have fun tonight. Don't think about finding a man. Do you," I said to myself.

As I made my way down the street, I saw that the parking lot was full. Valet parking was the only option, and I didn't want to pay for valet. I drove down the road and found parking along the street a few blocks up. By the time I parked, I had gotten over my little anxiety. I got out of my car, locked it, and walked to the House of Blues.

Thankfully, there was a separate entrance for those who were on the list. When I got up to the front, I gave my name and was let in.

On my way to the bar, I saw that Kaeja was mingling with Avian by her side. I waved. She waved back excitedly and headed over to me so Avian could finish having his conversation with some people.

"Bestie, you feel better now?" Kaeja asked with a huge grin. "My baby worked it out for you after all."

"Yes, I feel much better. Thanks, bestie. I didn't want to stay home by myself."

"I'm glad you're here. Raya, that dress came out hella cute! Showing much cleavage, and your back is all out. Okay, I see you. I can't wait to wear the dress you made me for your fashion show. You almost done planning for that?"

"Yeah, I am done with the planning stage. I gotta lock down the venue soon. I need a drink. Let me buy you a shot since you guys hooked a sista up tonight."

"Thank you. What we doing? Patrón shot?"

"Yup."

We approached the bar, found an open spot, and waited for the next available bartender. A busty, redheaded bartender came to us and asked, "What can I get you, ladies?"

"Let me get two double shots of Patrón and two lime wedges," I replied.

"Coming right up." She whipped out two shot glasses, poured two doubles, and retrieved two slices of lime. "That'll be twenty-two dollars."

I handed her $25. "Keep the change."

She nodded, and I handed Kaeja a shot glass and a lime wedge.

"We haven't had a double shot in forever," she laughed.

"I know. You ready?"

She nodded. We clinked glasses, down the shots, and chased them with a slice of lime. It was so smooth going down. That was why I loved Patrón shots.

"Whew," Kaeja said, setting the shot glass on the bar. "Jacoury's here." She nodded toward the entrance.

My heart stopped, and at that moment, it felt like the room was spinning as if I were on a sped-up carousel. "What? For real?"

"Yeah, he just walked in with some chick."

"A chick?" I snapped my neck, scowling.

"Mmm-hmmm." Kaeja shook her head. "Look at you."

"What?" I shot back defensively.

"Why you look like you smell something foul?"

I searched the room for him, ignoring her, but I couldn't see him in the crowd.

"Mmm-hmm. Like I thought," Kaeja continued. "You still want Jacoury."

I didn't respond. It had been five long years, but if he looked anything like he did before he went to prison, I didn't know how I was going to react seeing him face-to-face.

Kaeja laughed at the way I was still scanning the room. "This place is small, and he's so tall. I don't know how you don't see him. He's right there, wearing all white."

"I'm clearly blind as a bat, because I don't see him."

"Don't worry. He saw you, and he's headed this way. When you see him, you gon' lose your mind, aren't you?"

I fluttered my eyelashes and flipped my hair a little when I noticed a few guys giving me the eye. I felt sexy. "No, I'm not."

"Yes, you are." Kaeja laughed so hard.

I had sucked my teeth. "Whatever. I'm waiting on YoungGucci90 to hit me with a message."

Kaeja waved her hand at me. "Girl, bye. You and this online dating thing are too much for me. I wish you weren't up on there. You need to stop that and get your man back. You know you want to."

"He's not my man anymore. You said he's here with another woman, so he isn't thinking about me anymore."

Kaeja was acting like Jacoury and I were supposed to pick up right where we left off five years ago. Five years ago, we were juniors at UCLA. I had to try to get through the rest of college while he pleaded guilty to carrying an unregistered gun and not guilty to possession of cocaine. He had been riding with his friends when they were pulled over. He claimed the dope wasn't his, but the gun was. Nobody wanted to say whose dope it was, so he and his two friends wound up doing time. With a snap of a finger, his basketball career was over. To think he was so talented and could've really done something with his life.

Then it happened. I saw him, and it felt like I was being buried in cement. He was looking too good, and he was much more muscular than the last time I saw him. I didn't see the chick he was with at first, which made me want to run to him. I halted because she was right behind him, looking petite as an Asian with jet-black, straight hair. She was texting on her phone, not paying attention to anyone.

Jacoury and I locked eyes, and baby, my insides churned. I couldn't believe that he could still make me nervous. Kaeja wasn't lying when she said he was heading straight for us. There was no way I could get of it now. He was standing in front of us before I could blink.

"Wassup, Buttercup," he said, giving me that sexy smile.

I hadn't heard his little nickname for me in so long I almost forgot how it sounded coming out of his mouth. Looking him up and down, I bit my lower lip and replied, "Glad to see you finally among the free."

"You would've known when I'd be home if you visited a nigga, wrote a letter, or something. Shit, you ain't even pick up ya phone when I called. Ya moms came to visit me, though, but I'm sure you already know that."

I nodded. It used to irritate me that my mother went to visit him. I told her not to do that because it would give him false hope that things would work out. However, I couldn't stay mad at her, because she loved him like the son she never had.

"Hey, Jacoury," Kaeja said.

"Hey, Kae," he said as his six foot, eight inch frame towered over her for a hug.

I looked over at the chick, and she had stopped to talk to a few friends. She didn't seem to care that he was talking to us. She was that secure in her man, I guessed. She didn't seem to know who I was, which was cool with me because I didn't like drama.

Jacoury's eyes landed on mine again. My eyes traveled to his thick lips. They reminded me of the many times we kissed, but the memory of us kissing in the middle of a rainstorm outside the library in college took over. We were dripping wet and didn't care who was watching us.

I sipped my drink as the sweet memory slowly faded.

"Damn." He peered down at my outfit. "You lookin' good, Raya. I mean, you always look good, but that dress is . . . Damn. I can't even focus right now."

"Thanks. I designed it myself."

"Say less. That's dope as fuck. So you got your clothing line going?"

"Yup."

"That's what's up. You're living your dream, huh? I'm proud of you, baby. Congrats on everything you're doing." He reached out to hug me.

As soon as we hugged, I could feel his strong arms and washboard stomach through his shirt. A bigger grin covered his face. "It's really good to see you."

"It's good to see you too, buddy," I said, feeling jealous that he came with someone else.

"Buddy?" He chuckled at how that sounded.

"Yeah, buddy."

Jacoury tried to keep his body close to mine, but I stepped to the side, closer to Kaeja. He licked his lips and said, "You better be glad I got Tiff here with me tonight."

I scowled. "Is Tiff your girlfriend?"

"Nah, she's not my girlfriend," he said. "I mean, she held it down for me for the last few years. When I got out, she made sure I was straight. We see one another, but I got my own place, and she got hers. We haven't put a title on what we're doing yet."

I cleared my throat because I felt like he was trying to make me feel guilty. She had done for him what I couldn't handle. "Even if Tiff weren't here, what would that mean?" I asked.

"You and I both know what that would mean," he replied with a serious expression.

"You've been drinking tonight?" I quizzed.

"I don't drink, Buttercup. Stop playing. We got some catching up to do, though. Besides, I ain't tripping off you leaving a nigga hanging. I mean, you did say that if I had to do time, you wouldn't be able to do it, and I should've known you were dead ass. None of that matters now, though, 'cause I'm home, and I'm all yours if you want me to be."

I damn near shivered at the thought of his large hands palming my ass the way he did a basketball while giving me the hardest, deepest thrusts. This was my test. Had to be.

"Well, it is what it is," I said, playing him cool. "Welcome home. You have a good night with Tiff."

"To be honest, I wish I were spending my night with you. Is your number still the same?"

"Yeah."

"I'll call you later, and you better answer." He hugged me again, this time kissing my cheek. As he walked away from me, I could feel still feel his soft lips.

"Oh, my God," I said, exasperated.

Kaeja laughed at me. "You tried to play so hard earlier. I knew it! You still want him."

I shook my head and watched him as he rejoined Tiff. I couldn't help but wonder what things would've been like if I'd stayed down and done that time with him. Would we be married? Have children? I stared at them with a twinge of jealousy paining my gut, but I looked away to make the pain subside. I could have him if I wanted him, and he made that noticeably clear, but I wasn't going to play these games with Jacoury.

As I ordered a Patrón margarita, I did my best to ignore that my first love was in the same room with someone else. I drank while dancing to the music with Kaeja. She was keeping me company. The club was filling up, and unfortunately, women outnumbered men, as I'd predicted.

When was Chris Brown coming on? I was ready to see him.

As I spun around shaking my ass to the beat, two fine-ass men entered the building, one with lighter complexion than the other. They were the same height and had the swag of celebrities as they walked. The way they talked to one another had me staring.

Who are they?

Wait! The one with the caramel skin looked familiar. Was that Mr. YoungGucci90? If it wasn't, he sure had a twin walking around Los Angeles.

Oh, my God, what if that's him? I thought as I froze.

Kaeja said, "Raya, I'm going to VIP with Avian. Breezy's about to hit the stage in a little bit. Will you be okay by yourself? I hate to leave you."

I nodded. "Yeah, yeah, girl. I'm good. I'm about to keep sipping this drink." I didn't want to tell Kaeja that I thought I saw YoungGucci90, because I didn't need her freaking out.

"Okay," Kaeja said before walking across the room to join her man.

My eyes went right back to YoungGucci90's body double and his friend. His chocolate-covered friend had the most profound waves in his fade and diamonds over the tops and bottoms of his teeth as his smile was gleaming through the dim area. He was wearing a black, red, and white sports coat over a black Givenchy T-shirt, three gold ropes around his neck, black jeans, and black and red Air Force Ones.

I looked over at the doppelganger's attire and licked my lips slowly. He was wearing a black Gucci T-shirt, a

Gucci scarf hanging out of the back pocket of his dark blue jeans, and black Gucci loafers. He wore one single gold chain around his neck and a gold Rolex.

What they both were wearing couldn't be found at the Compton Swap Meet. They had dope boys' flair, but I didn't want to assume. They walked toward the bar, and I was in for a fight for my next breath, because up close, they were even finer.

Two women ran behind them, trying to get their attention. "Kyree!" one shouted. "Fendi!" the other exclaimed.

The chocolate one faced the women, saying, "Ladies, ladies. How y'all doing this evening?"

The caramel cutie ordered from the bar, "Let me get an Adios."

Mr. Chocolate kept talking as he put his arms around both women. He was charming the fuck out of them as the women seemed to be entranced by all that ice in his mouth. Mr. Caramel had his drink and joined in the conversation with his friend and the pretty women with the banging bodies.

I didn't want to interrupt and ask if he was YoungGucci90, because what if it wasn't him? I would feel embarrassed. I pulled out my phone to send a message through the dating website instead.

YoungGucci90 had responded to my message. I fumbled with my phone as it almost slipped out of my hands, but I caught it before it could hit the floor. I read:

Hey there, beautiful!

I had to pause for a moment because I'm trying to figure out if you're real. I looked through your pics, and you look like my type, but you might be too good to be true. Anyway, I'm 23 years old. I'm a single father to a 5-year-old son, whom I love to death. Why am I online looking for love? Well, I find that women don't like dating men with a kid, so it's hard out here for me. Please, if you don't want a guy with a child, it won't work, because he comes first in my life. I hope to hear from you soon.

Kyree

YoungGucci90's real name was Kyree. It was him! My heart was racing because I didn't know what to do next. I never dated anyone with a child before, so I didn't know how to feel about it. I hoped he wasn't the type to want me to meet his kid from the start. That would be too much.

I nervously hit reply and started typing:

Nice to meet you, Kyree. I think we're both at the House of Blues tonight. I'm wearing a dark blue dress, and I'm near the bar, literally a few feet away from you.

"Whoever has your attention must be special as fuck. You not ready to see Chris Brown?" a voice asked from behind me. The voice was deep, and it sounded sexy as it lingered around my eardrums.

I slowly turned around, and I was face-to-face with Kyree, aka YoungGucci90. His skin was so clear and smooth, blemish free. Those dazzling hazel eyes were staring through me.

"YoungGucci90, right?" I asked. "I mean, Kyree?"

He looked down at me with a slight frown as his eyebrows pointed down. Oh, his eyes were too beautiful.

"We know each other from online?" he asked.

I felt like fainting, but why? He wasn't some celebrity.

"Well, not really. We introduced ourselves this evening on Single Ready to Mingle. I'm—"

"You're Soraya. MissDesignDiva." A charming, bright white smile took over damn near his whole face.

"Yeah. That's me."

"Nice to meet you, Soraya. Beautiful name by the way."

"Thank you. Nice to meet you as well, Kyree."

"Yeah. It's funny, because I sent you a message on my way over here. Your pictures do you no justice. You take good pictures, but you look so much prettier in person, almost like a different person."

I laughed a little, making sure to flash him a quick smile as I blushed.

"You wearing one of your pieces? I clicked on your on-line store and checked you out. Boss chick shit. Your clothing line is pretty dope. I'm into fashion and shit too." He sipped his blue drink.

"Fashion and shit?" I giggled.

"Yeah," he replied.

"Well, I wear a lot of my designs. I have to be a walking advertisement."

"Always. You here alone or you waiting for whoever you were sending a message to?"

"Yeah. I mean, no. I was replying to your message. I'm here with my best friend and her boyfriend. They're over there in VIP."

"They didn't include you in VIP?"

"Nah, not this time. I got invited at the last minute." The way he was staring at me, it was hard not to smile so big, and he had my cheeks hurting.

"You should be in VIP," he said. He moved closer, and I recognized the scent of his cologne. He smelled like Gucci's Made to Measure, but I could've been wrong. I was pretty sure, because he was in Gucci from top to bottom.

"So the burning question is, why do you have a profile on the website? I'm sure you have a long line of niggas beating down your door, trying to see what's up."

"Not even close. I mean, I could be with someone, but I don't want to settle," I replied. "What about you? What you doing on there? You walking around here looking like some type of model. I saw those chicks flagging you down a moment ago."

A group of three young women walked by and said hi to him as if on cue. He threw up the peace sign with a nod and a charismatic smile. He had this friendly vibe, and I could see why he was so popular with the ladies.

His chocolate friend stood next to him, eyeing me as he said, "Damn, what's up, gorgeous?"

"Hello," I said.

"Young Gucc, who's this?" he asked.

"This is Soraya. Soraya, this is—"

"Fendi," he interrupted. "This you, nigga?"

"Could be."

"A'ight, well, I'll be over here." Fendi walked away.

Kyree laughed at the expression on my face. "Don't mind him. So about me, I promote parties and shit like this."

"You're a promoter? I saw you didn't specify much on your 'About Me' section."

"I would rather talk about me in a discussion, not on a page. If I laid everything about myself on a page, we would have nothing to talk about in person." He took out his iPhone X and showed me a digital flier for tonight's event. "King-Live Presents, that's me."

"Oh, okay. So you know Avian?"

"Avian Perez?"

"Yeah," I replied.

He nodded. "He works for Universal. How you know him?"

"He's my best friend's man. That's who I'm here with."

"Okay. Avian and I cross paths a lot." He stuck his phone back in his pocket.

"My best friend's been dating him since high school."

"Oh, okay. I never met her before, but he's constantly talking about her."

"They're super in love."

"I heard, but on some real shit, Avian could've gotten you up in VIP. He crazy for that."

I shrugged as I sipped my drink and realized I had come to the bottom of it. The straw made a sucking sound, and the ice clicked against the glass a bit.

"You want another drink before the show gets started?" he asked.

"Not right now. Thank you, though."

"No problem. Let me know when you need a refill. Let me put that glass up for you."

I handed it to him, and as he walked away to put the glass on the bar, I took a quick glance at how smooth his movements were. As good-looking as Kyree was, I expected him to be a little conceited, but he was the furthest thing from that. A cutie who didn't act like he was a cutie. I liked that.

My heels were starting to hurt my feet from standing. The only seats in the house were taken, and the open ones were in VIP. Damn it, I really wanted to sit down. When he returned to my side, I pretended as if my feet pains didn't exist.

"We only have a few minutes before the DJ cues Chris. You're so beautiful, you know that?" He bit his lower lip as his glassy eyes peered into mine.

"Thank you. You're quite handsome yourself."

"Thank you. Since you belong in VIP, let me get the best seat in the house. You look too good to be standing out here."

"Lead the way," I said.

Kyree took my hand into his, and we walked to the roped-off section.

Kaeja spotted me as we passed her. I read her lips as she said, "Who is that?"

I pointed to my phone, and I sent her a text.

Me: YoungGucci90!

I watched as she read her text. Her eyebrows were raised high in disbelief. I smiled to assure her that I was okay.

Kaeja texted: Be careful! Don't set your drink down!

I knew better than to do that. Kaeja may have watched too much news and scary crime shows about men slipping date-rape drugs into women's drinks, but she had a good point.

Kyree had a reserved area that was waiting for him, Fendi, and whoever else they wanted to join them. When I sat on the black leather sofa, my throbbing feet thanked me.

Kyree whispered over to some other dude who came into the section. The guy nodded and left. A waitress approached Kyree with a tray of ice, Cîroc, cranberry juice, and pineapple juice. Kyree winked at me and said, "You sure you don't want a drink?"

"I'll take a Cîroc and pineapple, please."

"I got you," he answered. I watched him closely while he made it for me.

"Wrist" by Chris Brown started playing, and everyone in the crowd got hyped up. Kyree handed me the drink as I nodded to the music. Chris Brown danced his way on the stage.

Chapter 4

Soraya

I was feeling myself. I had a drink and a couple of shots with Kyree and was at my limit. My feet felt numb past pain, so I took off my heels and put them on the side of the couch. I should've brought my little foldable ballet slippers, but I didn't think about it. My feet thanked me as they touched the shiny wooden floor.

Kyree moved up against my ass, his rhythm matching mine. I danced all up on him like he was already my man. I caught a few glances, some jealous stares. Women wished they were up there with him. I turned to dance face-to-face with Kyree, and he smiled at me.

I said in his ear, "I'm so glad I ran into you."

"Me too." Taking my hand, he turned me back around so I could grind my ass up against him. "You're wearin' the shit out of this masterpiece you created. I can tell you have a nice body underneath, the way I like."

"Yeah?"

"Hell yeah."

Breezy rocked the stage so hard he had the whole crowd grooving along with him. The energy in that place was through the roof. After a few more songs, Chris Brown was done. I felt a little sweat on my forehead. I wiped it with the back of my hand.

Kyree kept his body up against mine as he looked into my eyes. He rubbed his chin. "We should take a pic to remember how we first met."

"Okay," I replied.

He took out his phone and angled it up. I scooted closer so we could fit in the picture together. He snapped it, and our selfie was cute.

"Thank you," he said.

"No problem." I fanned myself a little bit because the mixture of the liquor and the warmth from everybody's bodies up in there had me feeling hot.

"There's gotta be a man out there trying to get your attention."

Was it that hard to imagine a woman like me could really be single? I answered, "Maybe, but I won't settle, period."

"Good. You shouldn't." Kyree's eyes ran up and down my body as if he were undressing me. "Did you enjoy the show?"

"Yeah, it was hella cool."

"That's what's up," he said. "Can I come home with you tonight?"

I laughed with my head slightly moving back. "You move a little fast, don't you?"

"No. Not at all," he replied. "What you doing after this?"

"I'm thinkin' 'bout hittin' up Jack in the Box drive-thru and sliding home," I said.

"Late-night Jack in the Crack run, huh? I feel that, but you should roll with Fendi and me to Buffalo Wild Wings or something."

"Nah, not tonight." I held my ground.

"Okay," he said. "Can I get your number?"

"Now I can do that."

After I had given him my number, I put on my shoes, and we headed out of the building. I looked around for Kaeja and Avian, but I didn't see them. He walked me to my car.

"I enjoyed kicking it with you tonight. I wish it wasn't ending already, but I'm sure we'll link up soon," he said.

"We will definitely."

I hugged him before I got into my car. As soon as I backed out of the parking space, my cell vibrated. I looked down to see an unknown number calling.

I answered, "Hello?"

"I see you made a new friend tonight," Jacoury said.

I recognized his voice instantly. "Don't even try it. You were there with Tiff, remember?"

"I'm taking her home and then I'm going home. You should come to see my new crib. See how I'm living."

My heart was pounding, daring me to go, but then I thought about Kyree. He was something new I was looking for. "Not tonight," I replied. "Maybe some other time."

He sounded disappointed as he said, "Okay. Save my number and hit me up anytime."

"I will. Night."

"G'night."

I ended the call and drove out of the parking lot to get some food. I got my spicy chicken sandwich with tomato, curly fries, and a small strawberry soda through the drive-thru, and I went straight home. I didn't even change out of my dress. I was that damn hungry. I kicked off those heels at the door, flopped down on the couch, and kicked up my feet. The pads of my feet felt raw like hamburger meat.

Avian and Kaeja walked in the door. Kaeja took off her shoes at the door and wavered on her feet.

"You cool, bae?" Avian asked her.

"Yeah, I'm gooooood," she slurred.

He shook his head and said to me, "Your girl is drunk."

"I see," I replied, eating some fries.

"I ain't drunk!" She was drunk because she was shouting instead of talking, which she always did when she was drunk.

He rolled his eyes and walked to her bedroom. She staggered over to me in her little tipsy walk before she flopped down next to me.

I laughed. "You good?"

"Shots, shots, and mo' shots, bitch!" she said. "Man, Breezy was so fuckin' lit. That nigga knows how to party. Wait, bitch, I saw you dancing all over YoungGucci90."

"He's so fine, ain't he?" I replied. "And those eyes."

"That part, and he wasn't checkin' for nobody but you. Avian knows him."

"Yeah, he told me that."

"How did he even know that you were there?" she asked with a scowl.

I sipped my soda. "He didn't know. I recognized him as soon as he walked in. I was kind of already tripping because he didn't hit me back after I sent him that message, and—"

She cut me off. "Hold the fuck up! Bitch, you sent him a message even though I told you not to?"

"Yeah, but anyway, girl, he is so dope. His name is Kyree."

"Yeah, Avian told me. You give him your number?"

"Hell yeah."

"Well, at least we know he ain't a catfish or a rapist or a killer. Well, I almost thought I would be waking up to see Jacoury sneaking up out of here. I would've been dying laughing at ya lying ass."

"Please. Even if I didn't meet Kyree in person tonight, Jacoury is a no go."

She rolled her eyes. "Yeah, okay. Don't act like I didn't see the way you two were gazing at one another."

"Take yo' ass to bed. Good night."

She laughed, "Night." She eased off the couch and sauntered to her bedroom.

My phone beeped. The battery was dying. I finished my food and headed to my room while turning off the lights. When I got to my room, I turned on the light and plugged up my phone. I got my laptop from under the bed and went on Facebook. I saw that I had a friend request from Young Gucci. I accepted and stared at his handsome profile picture. I scrolled through the rest of his pics to see ones that he didn't have on his dating profile. The images of him and his son running around the park were too adorable. The little man recently had a birthday at Disneyland. The pictures with Mickey Mouse were so cute.

I went down his timeline to see if there were any chicks posting anything or if he had baby mama drama. His baby mom had posted a few pics of their son playing in a swimming pool, and I clicked on her profile because I was nosy like that.

Her profile name was India. She was a mixed beauty with a bright smile. She was a shade lighter than I was, and her long hair looked real. I instantly felt a little jealous because of how pretty she was. Her relationship status said that she was in a relationship, but it didn't say who she was in a relationship with. My heart started beating fast. Her page was private, so I couldn't snoop the way I wanted to. I couldn't even see all her profile pictures.

I clicked back to his profile to see that his status said single. That made me relax. I lay on my bed and studied each profile pic to read the comments. He had a bunch of "you're sexy" comments but no responses to them.

A notification came through. I was tagged in the picture we had taken at the House of Blues. The caption read: She baaaaad, ain't she? My new friend.

I smiled. Wow, he was giving me Facebook love already. I was sure that the picture was going to piss off some of his followers. We looked cute together. I saved the pic in my photos.

A message popped up from him, and I was smiling so hard.

Young Gucci: You ain't in bed yet?

I replied: Nope. About to go to bed in a sec. What you doing?

Young Gucci: Why don't you call me and find out? 213-555-3211.

Chapter 5

Kyree

As the House of Blues cleared out, I waited for her call, growing impatient. Right before I could call her, Fendi walked up to me with a tall blonde on his arm.

"Ay, Gucc," Fendi said. "I'm about to leave with her. You good?"

"I stay good."

"A'ight. Bambi here is having an after-party at her crib. You rollin'?"

"Nah. Do you. I'm going home."

Fendi had been my A1 since day one. His mama named him Fendi. It wasn't some nickname because he liked Fendi. We met when I was promoting a summer jam for the radio station seven years ago, and we had been tight ever since. When you saw Fendi, you saw me and vice versa. We had so much in common: money, cars, hoes, ice. That was us.

"A'ight," he replied.

Fendi and I high-fived into a handshake and snapped fingers. That was the handshake we did whenever we greeted one another or left one another, something we had been doing for five years. I walked out of the House of Blues behind them but in the opposite direction to my car.

I got in and started it up. On my way driving to my crib in Watts, I looked down at my phone to see that Soraya still hadn't called me after I'd asked her to. I thought about calling her, but bugging a chick wasn't my style. I couldn't stop thinking about her, though. It was like she was the only woman in the club that night, and she made me feel like I was the only one she wanted as well. She could even stand on the other side of the earth, and I would still feel pulled toward her. I was drawn to her profile on the dating website alone, so to see her in the flesh really did something to me. There was something about her, and I felt like we could be the perfect match. I hadn't met a woman who made me feel this way in a long time.

Her mahogany brown eyes, her caramel skin, and her pretty face had me. The physical attraction was there without a doubt. I'd never seen her out before, and that was what intrigued me. Fendi loved entertaining the same bitches, but I was over that. They were still throwing the pussy like a nigga asked for it. I was on something new. Every word that escaped from Soraya's glossed lips was sexy as hell. I was ready to suck the hell out of those lips if she let me.

My cell rang and smiled. It was her.

"Hey. What happened?" I asked, unable to hide how impatient I was.

She giggled. "Sorry about that. I had to let my phone charge a little bit."

I smirked and let out a small chuckle as I pulled up into my driveway.

"What's funny?" she asked.

"Nothing, it's that I can't believe I'm feeling you like this already."

"Are you?" she asked.

I couldn't lie. She had my head reeling, my heart beating fast, and I couldn't wait to see her again. "Yeah. I really enjoyed my evening with you, which was the shit, by the way. You know how to have fun. I like that. Our connection is dead-ass amazing."

"You think so?" she asked, sounding surprised.

That perplexed me. Was I the only one feeling the sparks fly between us? I couldn't tell if she was playing a game with me, but I was about to show her that I didn't want to play games with her.

"I don't think so. I know so. Our chemistry is just like, wow. I can't describe it. I plan to make you all mine."

She laughed, but I was serious. I could see myself with someone like her. Fuck that, I could see myself with her. I was good at reading people. She was perfect. My approach was intense, to the point, and it may have been a little too early to put claims on her like that, but I was the blunt type.

"You want to make me all yours, huh? Before we get to all of that, tell me what you're looking for," she said.

"First of all, I'm not looking for anything, but when I meet the right woman, I plan to go all in. Everyone wants true love, someone who sets their heart on coast. Even though I'm a promoter, I'm not into chicks who are all up in the club all the time. I want someone to cuddle with at night, someone to hold hands with, and someone to chill and watch movies with. I guess you can say that I'm a hopeless romantic."

"I would say that you are, but nothing is wrong with that. Seems like you and Fendi are total opposites."

I chuckled. "Fendi and I are alike actually, but I'm changing. I'm getting tired of the same shit, feel me?"

"I hear you. What about your baby mama? How come that didn't work out?"

"Right to it, huh?" I rubbed the back of my neck, thinking of the right way to tell her my situation. "Well, it's a whole bunch of stuff. We fight over dumb shit. Once our son was born, it got worse. We both decided that we would chill out and not fuck around with one another. We're good friends when we get along, but that's about it. She's moved on, and so have I."

"Other than promoting, what else do you do?" she asked in her cute, soft, and gentle voice. I liked the way her voice sounded over the phone.

"I got my hands in a little bit of everything. I like to stay fresh, and that shit ain't cheap, so I would consider myself to be an entrepreneur."

"A hustler, you mean?" she tried to correct me.

"I definitely hustle, baby, but it's all legal. I'm not into illegal hustlin'. I've done enough time for that as is."

She paused as if the air had been sucked from her before she asked, "What you go to jail for?"

Damn. At that moment, I wished I hadn't said it. Now that it was out, I felt like I owed it to her to explain. As much as I wanted to move past this moment, I said, "I've gone to jail a few times, but that's in my past."

"For what?" she pressed.

Fuck! She wasn't letting up. I didn't want to say precisely what happened, but I was trying to do things differently. I was going to have to go there now that I'd brought it up. I bit my lower lip before I answered honestly, "Wasn't shit really. I was over in Arizona when I was nineteen, doing stupid shit with friends. I did a couple years. That was ten years ago, though, and I don't do shit I'm not supposed to anymore. Everything has been cool with promoting. I'm all about walking the straight and narrow now. You don't date niggas who been to jail or something?"

"No, I don't, but I appreciate you telling me."

"You sound like you ready to hang up in my face." I rubbed the back of my neck with my free hand.

She paused for a second, and I almost thought she hung up, but then she said, "I wouldn't hang up in your face. I would say goodbye first."

I felt like I'd ruined everything, so I tried to fix it by saying, "Well, I don't want to hide anything. You have plans tomorrow? How about we link up or something? It's Saturday, and I'm free all day. What about you?"

"Um, well . . ."

"Wait, don't tell me I scared you off." I closed my eyes and tapped the back of my head against the headrest a few times.

"No, um, it's . . . I have a few things I have to do, but how about you come by for brunch?"

Relief struck me as I opened my eyes. "You cook?" I didn't know any chicks in Hollywood who liked to cook. Eating out was the norm around these parts.

"Who said I was cooking?" she replied.

"Oh, my fault. You ordering takeout?"

She laughed. "I'm kidding. I cook. I guess I can cook brunch for us."

"You sure you from L.A.?"

"Born and raised. Why you sound so surprised?"

"How many women you know who cook around here? I'll wait. Nobody cooks like my Big Mama. Finding a woman who cooks is like trying to find a needle in a haystack around here."

She laughed. "Oh, I know what you mean. I got my cooking skills from my mama, and she doesn't play around in the kitchen. My mama is the best cook hands down."

"I heard the fuck out of that. What you going to cook for me? I haven't had a home-cooked meal in years."

"Years? That's a shame. You'll have to come over and find out. I'll call you in the morning." She yawned. "I'm so sleepy. Have a good night, Kyree."

"All right. You too, sexy. Night."

We ended the conversation. I turned off the car, got out, locked the door from my keychain, and walked up to the front door. I unlocked it and closed the door softly. I headed to the bedroom to get out of these club clothes. My phone chimed. I looked at it to see a text from Fendi.

Fendi: Fendi Bag, nigga!

I chuckled and shook my head. That was his way of saying that the chick he was about to fuck was a rich bitch. Los Angeles was full of women, but Fendi and I naturally attracted women with lots of dough.

Me: Say less, my nigga.

I tossed my phone on the dresser and got undressed before hitting the shower.

Chapter 6

Soraya

"Yesssss, Avian! Yes!" Kaeja screamed.

I rolled my eyes as my best friend's screams of pleasure came through my bedroom wall, preventing me from going to sleep. I hated that our bedrooms were right next to one another. We needed a house with bedrooms on opposite ends. Whenever Avian spent the night, Kaeja was guaranteed to scream and holler, but her moans seemed extra loud tonight for whatever reason.

I turned up my TV to help mask her sounds. *The Millionaire Matchmaker* on Bravo was on. It was an episode I had seen already, but I needed anything to cover up their noise. Plus I liked jotting down dating notes.

I thought about what I wanted to make for brunch since I'd volunteered to cook. Kyree's little confession about doing time almost sent me running. I instantly thought, *oh no, not another Jacoury!* But I decided to not let that bother me because it wasn't like he was fresh out. Now if he went back to jail, I wasn't going to fool with him.

"Kaejuhhhh . . . Shit!" Avian yelled before a loud thumping from the headboard proceeded to hit the wall.

Bang! Bang, bang! Bang!

"Oh, God," I sighed as I tried to bury my head into my pillow. Those two didn't sound like they would be finished anytime soon. It was going to be a long night.

Sleeping in the living room wasn't going to help either. This apartment was too damned small.

See, if I had a boyfriend, I would go to his place. I closed my eyes and imagined that my head was lying on Kyree's chest. I lifted my leg up to rest on another pillow as if it were his body holding me close.

Chapter 7

Kaeja

I rode Avian as if I were riding one of those mechanic bulls down at the pub and wore his ass out. I did not stop until he exploded. I lay next to him, and he couldn't move.

"Damn, baby," he said.

I laughed, "We gotta try to be quiet. Soraya is probably ready to kill us right now."

Our sex was too good to keep quiet. I did feel sorry for Soraya because she heard us every single time. She would complain, and the bags under eyes the next morning showed that she couldn't get much rest.

"She should be used to it by now," Avian replied with a shrug.

"It's not fair. If she had someone up in there, then I wouldn't feel so bad."

He sighed, "Well, we could be at my place, but you act like you don't like sleeping over there."

"It's not that I don't like sleeping at your house. I love sleeping in my bed, but I mean, if I lived at your place, it would be a different story."

He rubbed my back. "I hear you. We'll live together when the time is right."

"Okay. When the time is right, just know, my bed is much more comfortable than yours, so I'll be bringing it."

I was ready to move into his place, but he wanted me to wait for him to say when the time was right. Soraya could handle rent on her own, and we had already talked about it. My relationship with Avian was starting to feel stagnant. What was next for us? He never talked about marriage, and living together was something that he would say he wanted to do, but he wanted me to wait for him to say when that would be.

"I hear you," he said.

"Do you really hear me?" I raised one eyebrow as I gave him the side-eye.

"Yeah, baby, I know what you want to do. The day will be here before you know it. I've been thinking more about it lately."

Well, that was something new. He had never said those words before. I felt excited that I was breaking him down. I was ready to spend every day together.

"Have you thought of an exact date?" I asked. I wanted clarification so that I wouldn't get my hopes up thinking it would be by the end of the month.

He got out of the bed naked, ignored my question, went into my master bathroom, and closed the door to pee.

I sighed loudly and ran my hands through my curly hair. I was starting to become frustrated. Thirteen years of a monogamous relationship and not even a promise ring. Were we ever going to get married? I didn't know if he thought about marrying me, because he never brought it up and I never asked. I only hinted around, but he ignored me, much like he was doing at that moment, and I was really starting to wonder.

I picked up my phone from the floor and began scrolling through Facebook. That was when I noticed that a mutual friend, Lelee, had hit like on Avian's new profile picture. As I swiped left through his profile pictures, I saw that she had liked a lot of his profile pictures. We went to high school with this skanky broad, but I didn't know they were Facebook friends. When the hell did this happen? I sat straight up.

The fuck?

I wasn't in any of the pictures she'd liked, and it looked like she purposely skipped over them. I clicked on her profile and started reading her status updates. She'd posted a status the day before that read: Thanks for being such a good friend, Avian. I'm so lucky. Love you to the moon and back.

I scowled at my phone. Avian and I had had problems in high school with other chicks trying to say they were messing with him, but Avian would smooth everything over by saying nothing was going on. I was sure he would say the same about her, but when was he going to tell me that they were friends?

The toilet flushed. Avian washed his hands and came out of the bathroom. He collected his clothes one article at a time. He was getting fully dressed. That was weird to me. I noticed his phone was in his hand. *Was he on Facebook while in the bathroom as well?*

"You leaving?" I asked, sitting all the way up.

"Yeah. I'm going home to sleep in my bed."

"Really?"

"Yeah, really. You understand that, right? I feel like I need to sleep in my bed," he replied. He was hitting me with my own line. Why did he have an attitude suddenly?

"Oh. Okay. Are you saying that to be petty and start a fight? Your ass can usually sleep any damn where."

"Look, we had a good night, and now I'm going home. It's that simple. It's nothing for you to get all pissed over. I don't get mad every time you say you like your bed."

"You say you don't get mad, but I can tell it bothers you. Anyway, why is Lelee hitting like all over your page? Is she the reason you rushing up out of here?"

"What? Man, she's a friend. She can't hit like?" he replied with a frown. "That's what Facebook is for, isn't it? I mean, that's what I thought it was for."

"Since when have you and Lelee been this close?"

"Since high school. Listen, Lelee and I are cool. Aren't you Facebook friends with her too?"

"Hell no, and you know that! Lelee Harris gave you a special shout-out like 'thanks for being a friend.' Now that you acting all funny out of nowhere, I can't help but think something else is going on between you two."

He laughed as if I said something so funny. "Really?" He stopped laughing when he noticed I didn't think this shit was funny.

My chest heaved up and down as my breathing became heavier.

He put on his pants and came to the bed. Putting his arms around me, he placed a kiss on my forehead. "You definitely have nothing to worry about, baby. I'm all yours. Lelee was having issues with her car yesterday, so I let her use my AAA to tow her car. That's it. Now get some rest. I gave you that good dick, so you should be ready to go to sleep now."

"Yeah, good dick usually puts me right to sleep, but don't think that good dick has made me retarded. Why didn't you tell me that you helped her out?"

"It slipped my mind. I helped her and then rolled out right after. It's not even a big deal." He put on his shirt, slipped on his shoes, and gathered his duffle bag. "I love you. Hit me when you wake up."

He walked out of the bedroom, and I wrapped my body in the sheet to lock the door behind him. I marched back to my bedroom and closed the door. I flopped on the bed and picked my phone back up. I went back to Lelee's page and stalked it, but I didn't see anything else. Maybe what he said was true, but I still went to sleep pissed off.

Chapter 8

Soraya

I woke up around 8:00 the next morning, rolled out of bed, and brushed my teeth. I walked into the living room to see Kaeja on the balcony, painting a portrait while in her black kimono silk robe. Even though she did real estate for a living, her heart was in painting. She only painted now when upset as an outlet. She used to paint every day, but that was when we were in high school.

The colors of her painting of a woman were blue and black, very dark. I turned to look through her open bedroom door to see that Avian wasn't in bed sleeping. Usually, on Saturday mornings, they slept in. I thought I heard the front door open and close around three in the morning, but I thought I was tripping.

I smelled coffee, so I was sure she had already had a cup to help wake her up. Her hair looked as if she had been rolling around, tossing and turning all night without putting her silk bonnet on. I knew my friend all too well. Something happened between her and Avian.

Opening the glass sliding door, I stuck my head out and said, "Good morning, Kae. Beautiful painting. Kind of blue, though. You all right?" The sun was shining right in my face, but it felt good in the spring morning air. There was a little breeze, but it wasn't cold, and it felt good.

She faced me. "Giiiiiirl, I had a rough night. Avian went home before the sun came up."

"Why?"

"He claims he wanted to sleep in his bed."

"Wait, he used your line against you? Why? He spends the night when he comes over, so what made last night any different?"

"I don't know. Something ain't right. Not to mention Lelee had posted on her Facebook page about how much she appreciates their friendship, and the shit got under my skin. He helped her with her car by using his AAA."

"Wait, big-booty Lelee from high school?" I frowned.

"Yeah." She nodded.

"When did they become cool like that?"

"That's what I want to know! I don't get him. It's like he trips off my page all the time. Nobody can say shit to me, but that bitch can make a post, tag his name, and like every picture without me in it, yet I'm tripping."

"Whoa. That's not cool, Kae."

"I'm getting so tired of this shit. Why can't we live together, or better yet, how come he hasn't proposed?"

"You already know I think he doesn't want to live together, Kae. But I don't think Avian is dumb enough to mess around on you, especially not with Lelee. She ain't even cute like that. He's a nice guy."

"A nice guy with a touch of asshole right now."

"But that's what attracted you to him, the fact that he can be such an asshole."

Kaeja painted a little bit before tossing her brush into a bowl of water. "I'm about to come in. I'm done with this for now."

I backed up from the sliding door so that she could come in. She went straight to the kitchen, poured a cup of coffee, and added hazelnut creamer and sugar. I closed the screen door so that the fresh air could continue to sweep through our apartment.

I stood at the counter. "Yeah, I would say that you're pretty pissed off," I noted aloud while staring at her. "Have you talked to your mom and dad lately?"

She shook her head. "I wish I could talk to them, but things have not changed."

I nodded and decided to leave that subject alone. Ever since Kaeja dropped out of medical school, which they were paying for, and got her real estate license five years ago, her parents refused to answer her calls. Her father told her that he would never forgive her for ruining her life. She was the only child like me and felt as if her parents' harsh reaction was unwarranted. I didn't understand why they hadn't gotten over it by now.

"You should be able to talk to Avian about this situation with Lelee. You two should be able to communicate better by now, and you can't continue to sweep shit under the rug as if it doesn't matter. You get so upset, which you have every right to, but then move on as if you're not hurt. You wanted him to stay the night, and I bet you didn't even ask him to stay, did you?"

"I couldn't bring myself to do it, Raya. I feel like by now, he should already know how I feel."

"I feel you on that, but communication is everything. How else we supposed to get what we want? I'm sure he'll call you this morning and make it all better. I heard how you were screaming his name. At least he knows how to give you a real orgasm."

"That's never the issue," she said with sadness in her eyes. "I want more. I deserve more."

"We all deserve that fairy-tale shit." I didn't want her to start acting insecure, but as women, we knew when something wasn't right.

I didn't mean to change the subject abruptly, but I had to tell her that I had invited Kyree over. "Kyree is on his way. I'll be whippin' something up for brunch."

"You invited him over?"

I blushed a little with a shy grin. "Yes, I did."

"Oh, okay. I saw the picture he tagged you in on your page. Cute. I'll probably be here. If Avian calls to go to that mixer he put together, then I'll miss Kyree's visit. Damn, I don't want to drive myself crazy about this Lelee bullshit."

"Try not to sweat it too much unless Lelee's ass starts showing some true signs that something really is going on."

"Yeah. What time is Kyree coming?"

"I don't know. I gotta call him to see what time he wants to."

"What you gonna cook?" she asked.

"I was thinking about making my infamous peach upside-down pancakes, cheese omelets, grits, and some thick-cut bacon."

"Ooooh, that sounds so good. You puttin' them sugar-coated fried pecans on top of those pancakes?"

"Yup, you know it."

"Ooh wee, you throwing some shrimp into those grits, too?" she asked with wide eyes.

"You think I should?"

"Hell yeah!" she said. "Too much is never enough! I love it when you cook. Save some for me so I can eat it later."

"Okay, but don't you think cooking all of that will make him sprung before I need him to be sprung?" I scowled.

"Giiiiirl," Kaeja laughed. "Jacoury kept asking me who ol' boy was last night. I told him I didn't know. He should know better than to ask me about your business."

"He called me when I was leaving, wanting to see if I could see his crib. I politely declined. I'm about to throw on some clothes and go to the grocery store. You want to roll with me?"

"Um, I don't know. I really am sleepy. I didn't get much sleep at all."

"I bet. Well, I'll be back. You want anything from the store while I'm there?"

"Nah, I'm good."

Her Galaxy started ringing from the countertop. I looked at it and announced, "It's Avian."

She reached for it and picked it up. "Hello."

I knew he would call. Those two couldn't stay mad at one another longer than a few hours. I walked to my bedroom to throw on some sweats to get ready to head to the grocery store.

By the time I got back from the grocery store, Kaeja was leaving to go to Avian's. She should've taken her ass over to his house when he left last night. I noticed that she had cleaned up her paints and her coffee stuff. I didn't mind living with her because she was so neat all the time, and I was going to be sad the day Avian finally agreed to live together. I understood that she wanted to be with her man, and I couldn't blame her for that. If I had a boo, I would want to be with him all the time as well, but I didn't know what I would do here alone.

My phone chimed. It was a text from Kyree. He would be on his way over in an hour. I looked at the clock, and it was 10:30. I still had time to get dressed and start prepping the food. I was starving, and I wished I had eaten when I first woke up, but it was all right because I was about to cook in a bit.

I got in the shower, put on a light pink summer dress, and brushed my hair up into a ponytail. I put on a little bit of Honey Lust eyeshadow and mascara. I glossed my lips with Love Nectar gloss from MAC. I texted Kyree the address before heading to the kitchen to start prepping my food. I linked my phone with the Beats by Dre Pill that we kept on the kitchen counter. I played the R&B hits station from Spotify. I needed music when I cooked. It helped me stay in an upbeat mood, and if I was in a bad mood, the music cheered me up.

I must have lost track of time, because there was a knock on the door. I looked at the time, and it was 11:30 on the dot. He was prompt and on time. Damn, I didn't know anybody who went anywhere on time. I wiped my hands on a towel before going to the door.

When I opened the door, I shouldn't have been surprised by how good he looked in his Gucci fedora, black Gucci T-shirt, jeans, Gucci belt, and Giuseppes on his feet, but I was. He looked even better than he had the night before. His hazel eyes gazed upon mine as he pulled a bouquet of red roses from behind his back.

"Are those for me?" I asked with even more surprise in my voice. No one had ever given me flowers before. I didn't know what to do with them.

"Yeah, of course. Who else?" He handed them to me.

I took the roses from him and stepped back so he could walk in. "Thank you so much. Come in."

He walked in and looked around. "You got a lovely place. It's in a prime location down the street from Staples Center. I dig it. Is your roommate home?"

"Thank you. No, Kaeja's out with Avian. He has some industry mixer going on." I closed the door with a smile on my face. I placed the roses on the kitchen table and turned down the music a little. I went back to cutting some bell pepper. "Do you like shrimp and grits?"

"I had some at Pappadeaux when I went to New Orleans for the Essence Fest last year," he replied as he came to sit on a stool so he could watch me work. "You telling me you can make it that good?"

"Hell yeah! Now I've had theirs, and it's good, but wait 'til you have mine. Mines is slammin'."

He came off the stool and approached me. He wrapped his hands around my waist with ease and pulled me close, causing me to drop the knife on the cutting board.

"I think you might taste better," he uttered.

My eyes grew wide as this throbbing instantly starting going on between my legs. The anticipation of feeling his tongue on me had me ready. Our chemistry was undeniable. I was wet like that. I took a deep breath as I tried to control the wild sensations that were attempting to make me rip off all his clothes.

"Matter of fact, I bet you taste even better," he said.

"Oh, really?" I raised my eyebrow.

In one quick motion, he lifted me up off my feet and moved me to a countertop that wasn't occupied by my ingredients for me to sit. I tried to steady my breathing for what was coming next. Kyree kept his eyes on me the entire time as he gently spread my legs apart. I sucked in a mild breath when I felt him ease off my wet thong. Lord, I didn't mean to be so wet, but the sight of him had me feeling like a waterfall.

"Mmm-hmm," he moaned as he stared down at my wetness. "I like how wet you are." He flashed me a perfect smile before he pushed my legs even farther apart, making my dress slide up above my hips.

He lowered his body down to his knees. Now I'm not going to lie. My first thought was, *I can't believe this dude is going down on me already.* He didn't know anything about me or if I got around like that. How many times had he done this before? The next second, his tongue was making rings around the opening of my pussy. He felt so good that my questions flew right on out of my head.

I could hear Kaeja calling me a nasty ho, but I pushed that out. Who was I turn down some good-ass head like this? If I was a tramp, then so be it. I was straight trampin'.

Kyree had me feeling like I was climbing up that counter, and I had nowhere to run. My head rested against the cabinets, and I closed my eyes tight as he licked deeper. He palmed my ass so my pussy could cover his entire face. I moaned while he sucked and licked at my inner folds as if I were the best-tasting thing he had ever eaten. He gripped my ass tighter and used his tongue to twirl and twist like a tornado in the middle of a storm.

I couldn't take it. To fight off the feeling of a massive orgasm, I tried to push him away, but he didn't dare stop. He stuck his tongue so deep inside me that I let out a loud sound. I grabbed his Gucci fedora and threw it on the kitchen floor. I pulled his head so his tongue could reach deeper inside me. Arching my back, I went ahead and let that orgasm happen.

The orgasm came and washed over me like a wave upon the shore as I couldn't fight it anymore. He lifted himself up enough to slip two fingers into me as he used his tongue to tantalize my clit, and I exploded. I shook with such force that I thought I was about to fall off the counter. My mouth was parted open, and my sultry moan was thick and full of the air I was desperately trying to catch.

"Mmm-hmm," he moaned as he continued to suck gently on my clit, licking my juices that were seeping out.

I came hard, and he eased me off the counter.

"Like I thought. You taste too damn good. Where can I get cleaned up?" he asked.

"Down the hall on your left," I replied, out of breath and feeling flustered.

He winked before disappearing down the hall. I had never come that many times from oral sex. He had set my body on fire, and I wanted more, but now wasn't the time. We were moving way too fast.

I quickly rushed to Kaeja's bathroom to wipe myself down, and I cursed at myself under my breath for giving in to temptation. By the time I went to my room to put on a new pair of panties, Kyree had helped himself to my kitchen. He was finishing the prep work by chopping up the rest of the bell pepper and onion.

I cleared my throat as I joined him in the kitchen. "What you think you doing?"

"I'm good at prepping. So I'm gonna be your sous chef this afternoon." He had chopping skills as he quickly got my veggies together.

"Wow, okay. I wasn't prepared for that."

"Looks like you weren't prepared for a lot of things today," he said with a sly, sexy grin. He wasn't lying, because his tongue shocked the hell out of me.

I picked up his hat from the floor and placed it on the counter. "Thank you, baby," he said.

He called me baby as if it were so easy to say. I blushed a little as I took the package of shrimp out of the sink. I started removing the tails and tossing them in the trash.

I had glanced over at him. I couldn't believe that Mr. YoungGucci90 was here in my kitchen cooking with me, but more than that, that he had given me one hell of an orgasm.

Chapter 9

Kaeja

"When can I move in?" I asked Avian as soon as I entered his house.

He sighed loudly as if he was sick of me asking. "Baby, I get how much you love your bed, and I'm sure you want to bring it here. I don't want to get rid of mine."

"Fuck you, Avian!" I yelled at the top of my lungs. "You be on that straight bullshit!"

His deep scowl and raised eyebrow were a warning. I had never talked to him like that before because I'd never had to. Why wouldn't we toss his mattress out and use mine? Of course I would bring my bed if we lived together. He'd never made this much fuss over my bed before, so I didn't know where his new little funky-ass attitude came from. I was beyond frustrated.

I watched him while he calmly walked across his living room to his balcony, which overlooked Venice beach. He didn't like it when I cursed at him, but that was the only way for him to know that I wasn't playing around with him.

"Watch your mouth, Kaeja. I'm serious. You don't need to talk to me like that. We will make the arrangements when the time is right. Right now, I will not discuss living together."

I narrowed my eyes at him. He'd completely changed from the young man I fell in love with at Sherman Oaks

High. Even as the most popular dude in school and captain of the football team, he was sweet to me. Never in a million years would I have thought we'd be fighting so much. I knew he had asshole tendencies, but he wasn't that way with me until now.

"I hate when you brush off this conversation," I whined as I grabbed my clutch.

"Let's go," he said, refusing to keep this topic going.

He was ready to take me to the industry mixer he'd put together. He loved networking, and it was necessary for the kind of business he was in. I loved being around my man, but I really wasn't feeling hanging out in front of others when our vibes were off-kilter. I was sure there would be a lot of people around, so we really wouldn't get to hang out together. There would be too many thirsty-ass chicks around, but he loved the attention. Our relationship was starting to rip at the seams. We hardly spent any time alone unless we were fucking or sleeping. I couldn't continue to live this way.

Once inside his car, Avian was silent.

"What is your . . ." I started to ask him what was on his mind, but I decided not to push any more buttons. "Never mind."

He didn't say a word, as if he hadn't heard me at all.

Avian walked into the club with a smile plastered on his face as if we hadn't been in an argument. He was the man everybody was waiting to see. I walked in beside him with a fake smile. The place was packed as it always was when he threw his events. I didn't usually feel insecure, but since Avian was acting so strange and walking with space between us, I couldn't help it.

I stepped farther inside and walked over to the bar to order an apple martini, keeping my eyes on my man. Two women, wearing skimpy spandex dresses, walked toward Avian. One of them had green contacts and long, jet-black hair that extended all the way down to the curve of her ass. The other had a blond wig on. She licked her lips once she was standing in front of Avian. *When did this type of shit start happening? Or did I not notice before?*

I decided not to order my drink yet, walked right on over, and stood beside him.

"Kaeja, this is one of Universal's newest artists, Unique," he introduced us.

"Hello," I said without a smile.

She didn't say hello in return. Unique was smiling at me, but I saw how she looked me up and down before he introduced us. "Will you be in the studio later?" she asked him.

Some woman with a short bob was looking at Avian as if he were a piece of delicious fruit. I didn't know what these bitches were doing, but the jealous girlfriend in me was surfacing.

"I won't be in the studio tonight," he said gently. "If you need to set up a time for a meeting, contact the office, and they'll put you down."

Unique shot me a strange look before flipping her hair and walking away with her sidekick.

"The fuck was that about?" I asked, eyeing Avian.

He shrugged his shoulders. "I don't know. I'm here on business, so let me work. Go get you a drink or something. I don't need you to babysit me." Before I could reply, he walked away toward another group of folks.

I walked back over to the bar, trying to hide my embarrassment. I could've stayed home for this shit, but I was hoping things would get better between Avian and me. I wanted to be with him, and I didn't want to go home. I ordered a few apple martinis and took my time drinking them alone. I waited to see if Avian would join me. I scanned the area, but I didn't see him because he had gotten lost in the sea of people.

"Kaeja?" a female voice behind me asked.

I turned around to face Lelee. I instantly scowled. What the hell was she doing here?

She had on a white dress that had this see-through material in her cleavage area. The last time I checked, Lelee wasn't in the music industry. She was looking at me with her eyebrows raised. She seemed surprised that I would even be there. Why wouldn't I be?

"Hey, girl," she said in the fakest tone as if we were the best of friends.

I wasn't going to hide my distaste for her or act phony. "What you doing here?"

"Avian invited me," she said through her smile.

"Oh, really?"

"Yes, really."

Now I really was pissed. Before I could yell Avian's name, he was approaching us.

"What's up, Lelee? Glad you were able to make it." He spread his arms and pulled her in for a hug.

She hugged him, and I cleared my throat loudly. I cocked my head to the side and looked at him sideways.

"Why you looking at me like that? I know you ain't trippin'," he said in front of her, and it caught me off guard.

I fluttered my eyelashes and pulled him to the side, away from her ass. She sashayed off and went to the bar to talk to one of her friends. This whole little messy scene wasn't making any sense to me. I felt like I had stepped into a bad episode of one of those reality shows.

"I'm trippin' because you invited her without fucking telling me. Something's not right. It doesn't add up, Avian. First, you helped her with her car, using your insurance unexpectedly, and then bam, here she is at your mixer. What the fuck is really going on? Don't lie to me!"

"She's a friend. Stop it. I only invited her to be nice. After I had the car towed for her, she mentioned that she doesn't get out much. To fill the place up, I went ahead and asked her to come. She ain't nothing to me and won't be anything, so stop acting so goddamned insecure."

He pulled me to him, and I felt my attitude leaving. "What's gotten into you, baby? Please don't do this here, okay? I'm sorry about last night. You and I need to do better and talk about our feelings."

"Okay, Avian, but I wish you could've at least given me a heads-up."

He ran his hand up and down my back. "That's my bad, baby. For real, I'm sorry. Did you get your drink?"

"Yeah, I had a couple. Are you drinking?"

"Nah, I'm going to drive us back to my place as soon as this is over. You staying the night tonight, right?"

I needed to get over the petty thing about not sleeping in my bed because it was more comfortable, since that bothered him. "Of course, baby. Your bed is my bed too."

He nodded as if that was the answer he wanted to hear. "I love you so much. Thank you for understanding," he said.

Before I could respond, we were interrupted by Lelee and her friend. "Hey, Avian. Where's the bathroom?" Lelee asked as she looked around.

"Yeah, uh, it's right around that corner," he replied.

Why in the world was she asking him where the damn bathroom was? There were all these other people around here, and she had to ask him?

Avian read my expression as the two of them walked away. "Don't do this with her." He gave me a stern look.

"That bitch is trying me."

"I'm serious, Kaeja. Don't go there. I've worked too hard to pull this mixer together. I can't have no drama fuckin' my shit up."

I sighed heavily. This was going to be a long-ass day. "Okay, I hear you. I'll stay on the opposite side of the room, and if I see her coming, I'll avoid her."

"That's my baby." He gave me a soft kiss on my lips.

Chapter 10

Soraya

It was Kyree's grand idea to eat brunch at the park. Everything was cold by the time we got there, which I predicted, but he was insistent. I had everything packed in a cute wicker basket, and we ate on a blanket on the grass underneath a big, shady tree. Though the food was cold, we enjoyed it. Our afternoon was romantic before he started having a sneezing fit and our afternoon quickly became an allergic person's worst nightmare.

"Kyree, are you all right?" I asked after he sneezed for the fifth time.

"Yeah, I need some Benadryl or something. I didn't think this out all the way. I'm sorry."

"If you are allergic to grass and pollen, why would you suggest coming to the park?"

"I wasn't even thinking. I'm embarrassed."

"Don't be embarrassed. I have allergies too, but I take Flonase and Claritin, especially around spring. I have some Claritin at home. You want to leave and get some?" I asked.

"Nah, I have some in the car."

He hopped up and went over to his car. He looked through the glove compartment, and he came back with a box of Benadryl and a small package of tissue. He popped a few pills in his mouth and downed them with what was left in his water bottle.

"Well, at least you have something to relieve you. Now you're about to be sleepy. Benadryl always knocks me right out."

"Not me. It's the only thing that works. I try to keep it around since I'm constantly on the go. It's not hot having a runny nose and shit."

I giggled. "No, that's not hot at all."

He chuckled, but then turned serious after he blew his nose. "What did you really think about the event at the House of Blues? You can be brutally honest."

"The show was lit, and he could've stayed on stage a little bit longer. I know it wasn't a full concert, but a little more time would've been perfect. You have any more shows lined up?"

"Not yet. I'm trying to book the Migos and Cardi B."

"Ooooh, that would be lit too," I said.

"Yeah, I'm trying to keep the nightlife lit around here." He blew his nose again and balled up the tissue.

"I saw on your dating profile that you work on cars. Is that another job or hobby?" I asked.

"Both," he replied. He looked so cute with his red nose, looking like he could audition to be Rudolph the Red-Nosed Reindeer for a Christmas play. Even though he was suffering from his allergies, he was still handsome.

"Come here," he said, biting his lower lip.

I leaned over to him. He kissed me softly. We parted, and he said, "Did I tell you how fine you are today?"

I giggled, "No."

Kyree kissed me on my cheek and planted more down my neck. I closed my eyes and enjoyed his kisses. He placed his hand gently on my face and kissed me deeper and harder. We were so wrapped up in our kisses that nearly forgot we were in the park.

"I'm ready to get out of this park," he said. "You?"

"Yeah, where you want to go?" I asked. I was curious to see where he lived. Kaeja said that if a nigga avoided going to his spot, that meant he either lived with his mama or another broad.

"You want to come to my place?" Kyree asked with his eyebrows raised. "I live in the hood. It's not upper crust like your spot."

I laughed. "Upper crust? I don't mind the hood. At least you got your own spot. My mom was born and raised in South Central," I replied.

"Really? I would think you were from Ladera Heights or something."

"Why, because I'm bougie?"

He laughed. "Nah, I don't think you're bougie. I made a dumb assumption, so please don't take it personally."

"I don't. Well, I guess you can say I've heard it before. My mom lives in Baldwin Hills, but we didn't move there until I was eight years old. What about you?"

"I was born and raised in Watts with my grandmother. My parents weren't around like that. They got lost in the sauce of pimpin' and hoin' and died that way. Big Mama passed away a while ago. She left me some money, so I bought my house with it. We could go to my house, but it definitely won't be all that private."

"Why wouldn't it be private? You and Fendi stay together?"

"Nah, Fendi got his own spot. My son is at home, and my cousins are staying with me temporarily until they find a spot. My cousin, his wife, and their six-year-old daughter recently moved here from Alabama. So . . ."

I wanted to be alone with him, and I wasn't sure if Kaeja was on her way home, but I wasn't in the mood to meet his cousins. "Okay, well, we can go back to my place. I'll visit your place some other time."

"Cool," Kyree said. "I'm down for that."

"A'ight, let's go."

We cleaned up our brunch, throwing away our plates into the trash and putting everything back into the little wicker basket.

When we got to the apartment, Kaeja hadn't made it back yet. I put the basket on the counter while Kyree made himself comfortable on the couch. He yawned.

"You tired?" I asked as I sat next to him.

"A little bit." He put his arm around me, and I cuddled up next to him.

"That allergy medicine must be kicking in. I told you it would make you sleepy."

"I feel a whole lot better, though. What's up with those lips?" He stared down at me.

I didn't hesitate to kiss him. Right in the middle of a lot of tongue action, his cell phone rang from his pocket.

"I gotta get this. One second." He answered it, hopping up from the couch as if it were an emergency call. "Hello. Yeah, all right. I'm on my way." He ended the call and said, "I gotta go. My son keeps asking when I'm coming home. I promised I would buy him a new video game today, and he's too anxious to wait."

"Oh. No problem."

I stood up, and he embraced me. He lifted my chin with his fingers after we parted. "I'll give you a call later, okay?"

"Okay. I'll be waiting."

He kissed my lips passionately. I felt a little disappointed because I wanted to hang out with him for a bit longer. Now I was going to have to find something to do in my free time.

"I had a good time," he said.

"Okay. I enjoyed you too."

I walked him to the door. He gave me one last kiss before he left. I sighed and went to the picnic basket to unpack everything. I put the dishes in the sink and put the leftovers in the refrigerator. I linked my phone to the Beats Pill and got busy washing the plates.

Afterward, I sent my mom a text to see if she wanted to hang out and watch Lifetime movies or something. My mom didn't like talking on the phone a whole lot, so the best way to get her attention was through text messages.

Mommy: Come on. I'll whip up some snacks.

I disconnected my music, grabbed my keys, phone, and purse, and was out the door.

I walked into my mother's house in Baldwin Hills, using my key. This house was the house I grew up in. As I walked down the wide hallway, upon the walls were photographs of me as a baby, some of me playing soccer, my high school and college graduation photos, and pictures of us together.

As soon as Kae and I got our apartment, she had hardwood floors installed. This two-story house had always been too large for us, four bedrooms and three bathrooms, but this was her dream house. She was a successful lawyer, and this house was a trophy of her success.

I walked toward the back of the house to the kitchen, guessing she would be there since she mentioned whipping us up some snacks. My guess was right, because she was standing at the kitchen island, sprinkling mozzarella cheese on two mini pizzas. I noticed the flour on the counter, which meant she made the dough from scratch.

"Hey, Mommy."

"Hey," she said, picking up the baking sheet to put the pepperoni pizzas in the oven. "What you up to, pumpkin?"

I hugged her, and she kissed my cheek. Everyone said that my mama reminded them of Clair Huxtable from *The Cosby Show*. I understood why they thought so. She was beautiful, just like her, intelligent, driven, funny, and no-nonsense when it came to her only child. She was a talented family lawyer. My mother valued the importance of maintaining a successful career and a stable household at the same time.

She met my father in college. They didn't date until after law school. They never got married even after I was born. They tried living together until I was 3 years old, but he cheated, married a white woman, and moved to New York. I never saw him again. I didn't know if he had other children, and I didn't care to know. My mama was all I needed.

"I went on a picnic date in the park today," I said, pulling out the stool to sit on.

"With Jacoury?" she asked with a sly grin.

She was so mad that I broke up with him that she stopped talking to me for a few days. From day one, Jacoury was in my mama's good graces. He could do no wrong. I was my mother's only child, and it was like she really considered Jacoury to be one of her children, which was so weird to me. I was almost afraid that if I met someone else, she wouldn't like him as much as she liked Jacoury.

I laughed. "No, Mommy. I met someone new last night."

"Really?" she asked, looking and sounding disappointed.

I sighed. "Mom, you have to let the idea of Jacoury and me go."

She looked into my eyes with a slight smile on her face. "I don't really want to, but if you want me to, I will. Just know I'm silently rooting for Jacoury. You want a berry smoothie?"

"Yes, that sounds good."

"This will be the best berry smoothie you ever had in your life," she said, going into her stainless-steel Samsung smart refrigerator. She took out strawberries, blueberries, and blackberries, and set them on the island. "Jacoury's been by here since he got home. I thought I'd tell you that."

"He told me, and I'm sure you talked about me."

"Yes, of course we did, but not in a bad way. He still loves you."

"Hmmm. Did he tell you about his new girlfriend?"

"She's not his girlfriend," she corrected in his defense. "She's a good friend of his."

"I guess. Mama, why did you continue to visit him while he was in jail?"

"It's a no-brainer really. Just because you stopped loving him doesn't mean I had to. I love that young man. He made a mistake, and after looking into the details and lack of evidence of his case, I was able to get him off. Those drugs weren't his. It was his first and only time ever in trouble. You didn't have to be that hard on him."

I should've known that she was going to help him out of that situation. The lawyer in her wouldn't let him stay in jail like that. She would've done the same thing for me.

"Well, it's done now. He can move on with his life, and I can move on with mine. I ran into him last night at the House of Blues. He was there with that girl."

She put Greek yogurt into the blender and added soy milk. "Did you speak to him?"

"I did."

"And were you nice?" she questioned.

"I was nice, Mommy. Anyway, I want to talk to you about the guy I just met."

"Okay."

"He's a party promoter, and he has a son—"

"He's got a baby?" She raised her eyebrows at me while she turned on the blender. She waited until she was done blending before she asked, "You ready to be somebody's stepmom?"

"I wouldn't say that I'm ready. I'm not thinking that far ahead."

"Well, if you date a man with a child and it works out, that is what you will become."

"I'm taking it one day at a time. The boy has a mother, and he's a good father from what I can tell. I do not think that deeply, but it's in the back of my mind."

She poured the smoothies into two tall glasses and placed purple straws in them. "How's Paradise You coming along?" she asked.

"Good. I'm so excited about the fashion show coming up. I finally have a collection done."

"I cannot wait to see everything you've been working so hard on. I'm really proud of you, pumpkin."

"Thanks, Mommy."

"Okay, while I make a salad, go find us a movie to watch on Netflix. The pizzas will be done shortly."

"No problem." I eased off the stool with my smoothie and went into the family room.

Chapter 11

Kyree

My baby mama, India, was sitting on my couch, scrolling through Instagram while Kai was playing *Minecraft* in front of the TV when I walked into my house. I was pissed because her emergency really wasn't an emergency at all. My eyes went straight to the empty wine bottle and glass on the coffee table.

India looked a lot like the cartoon Pocahontas, and it wasn't because of her partial American Indian heritage either. Her long hair, almond-shaped eyes, and skin tone were what did it for me when I first met her. She was beautiful in her own right, but what we used to have couldn't be repaired. Although she was supposed to be moving out, she conveniently didn't have anywhere to go. We agreed that I would do my thing and she would do hers, so I didn't know why she couldn't chill out. Every couple of days, she was sweating me about my whereabouts as if we hadn't already verbally agreed that we were done.

Okay, so I lied to Soraya when I told her my cousins were staying with me, but I didn't want to come out and say that my baby mama hadn't moved out yet. I had love for India, but I didn't want to be with her, and I couldn't put her out on the street, because she really didn't have anywhere to go. The only family she had was her mother, but her mother was married to an alcoholic.

"Where the hell you been? I've been calling you all day," India said.

I headed to the kitchen to get a beer, refusing to answer, and she followed me.

"Ky, who is this bitch you all hugged up with on your Facebook page?" She held up her cell phone to show me the picture as if I hadn't taken the photo myself.

I popped the top of the Blue Moon and drank. India knew better than to question me, but I already knew that posting that picture would stir up some shit. I really didn't give a fuck anymore, and I hoped this would be the moment she said she was moving out.

"It ain't no big deal, but it really shouldn't matter all like that."

Her eyes were wide as they filled up with tears. "That's your muthafuckin' problem. You always think shit ain't a big deal. How you think this makes me feel, Ky? Your damn dick still wants to poke around when you need to be figuring out how to fix your family. I swear, I hate you sometimes."

I gulped the beer and stared her down. She was going to have to watch her tone or else she was going to have to deal with me in a way she didn't want to. I never hit her. That wasn't my style. I merely left when I needed to, and she didn't want that because I would head right to the same bitch's house she was talking shit about. India hated to lose me to anyone. I stepped outside of our relationship, and she still hadn't gone anywhere. She hated the thought of the next bitch sucking and fucking me but would stay and be tortured to make me unhappy.

She narrowed her eyes at me before rolling them. "Why you all hugged up with her in this picture? I told you I would leave if you keep doing this shit to me!" she exclaimed.

"Good! So why you haven't bounced yet? I'm waiting for you to leave."

"That's too bad 'cause I'm not going anywhere. What's it going to be this time with this one? You plan to use her for her credit? Money? You want another car? This gotta be part of one of you and Fendi's womanizing schemes."

"You got me fucked up. I told you I'm done doing that shit. Plus I don't know why you tripping when I put money in your hands to do whatever you want," I reminded her. "Look, I don't use women for come ups anymore. Hurting and using women ain't my style."

"It ain't? You use me and hurt me, though. You're such a bad liar. Were you with her today? Was that why you went MIA for a few hours?"

She should've known that I wasn't going to answer any of her fucked-up questions. I didn't want to take advantage of anyone. I couldn't help it if broads offered to buy me shit. I could buy my own things, and I had a closet full of Gucci everything that I bought myself.

Silly tears fell from her eyes. The wine had her emotions all over the place. Every time she talked about other bitches and me, she cried. By now, India should've understood her role in my life. I was her baby daddy, and that was all. Any woman who had ever been with me knew exactly what that meant. Some days, I came home late. Some days, I didn't come back at all. India was the one who was home, waiting for me to return after my sexual escapades. It didn't matter how much she yelled, cried, or screamed at me, I was going to go wherever I wanted and do what I wanted. If she had moved out already, she wouldn't have to go through this.

"Well," she said after a minute or two of silence, "I told you not to have bitches all over your Facebook, Ky. I already allowed you to change your status to single, and I even deal with you not wanting me to tag you in pics unless it's your son in them. You told me that you wouldn't put your shit in my face if I'm here. I understand that you can't keep your dick in your pants, but you could at least have some fucking respect for me as your son's mother!"

I set the beer on the counter and softened up toward her. She was right. My indiscretions weren't for her to see. I held out my arms, and she wasted no time coming to them. "India, listen, I'm sorry, but we gotta figure something out."

"Why can't you love me and only me? I don't know any other woman who would tolerate what I tolerate with you. I'm not even gonna start on all the bullshit Fendi gets you into. Whoever this bitch is will be dumping ya ass when she finds out how y'all really get down."

"Now you talking crazy. How do I get down? Tell me. You never had to pay a bill. I bought everything you own, and I keep my son shining. You over here sounding like a bitter-ass baby mama now that I cut you the fuck off."

"Call me whatever you want, but I'm not stupid. Your womanizing ways will catch up to you, Ky, and when they do, I'm gonna laugh my ass off."

"Listen, I'm only going to say this to you one more time. I won't bring anybody to this house because this is where you lay your head. If you need me to help you find a spot, let me know, but you gotta go. Point blank period."

"I don't need help looking for a spot. I need help paying the rent. You going to give me enough child support to cover it?"

"I will, but how's the job hunt coming along?"

She rolled her eyes and walked back over to the couch, which was where she had been sleeping ever since we decided to split. India was wrong about me. My intentions with Soraya weren't what she thought. I was really looking to settle down, but with the right one. If Soraya was the one, I wasn't going to treat her the way I had treated India.

I went into the living room and said to Kai, "Hey, son. Let's go get that new video game you want."

"Yay!" He pushed pause on his controller and jumped to his feet. He opened the door, and I followed him to my car.

Chapter 12

Soraya

The next morning, I got up and checked my phone. I had come home from my mom's house late because we fell asleep watching *The Notebook*. I texted Kyree, but I hadn't gotten a response. I took a shower, had some eggs and bacon, and started designing at my design table.

"Soraya," Kaeja sang as she came out of her bedroom.

I had slipped off into a soft daydream about Kyree, and I hadn't even realized that Kaeja was home. Not hearing from him was bothering me. I didn't like to be ignored, but I wasn't going to sweat him. We were getting to know one another, and I didn't want to act like that crazy girl who couldn't take a hint. He would call if he wanted to talk to me again.

"When you get home?" I asked.

"I got home this morning," she said. "I slept in Avian's bed. He had to go run some errands this morning, so I came home."

"You slept in his bed? I bet that shocked the hell out of him."

"Yeah, his face looked like yours right now." She laughed. I laughed with her. "We finally talked some more about me moving in," Kaeja said. "I mean like really talked about it. It's going to happen soon."

"Oh, yeah? When you moving?"

"He said in a couple months."

"Whoa, that's some serious progress. Are you happy about that?"

"I'm ecstatic. He even talked about where I would put my clothes. We're going to buy some new furniture, including a new bed that will be ours."

I smiled at her, but I couldn't help but feel sad about it. I mean, it was about time that Avian agreed to move to the next step in their relationship. How could I not feel a little disappointed that she was would be leaving me to live alone? We knew this day would come, so I didn't understand why I was feeling this way.

"Congratulations," I said.

Kaeja's eyes were sparkling, and she looked so happy. I hoped Avian was serious because I didn't want to see my friend hurt.

There was a knock on the door, so I left my design table and walked over to the door. Once I looked out of the peephole to see who it was, I gasped. It was Kyree, and he was standing there looking fine with some sunglasses on. *Why didn't he call or text before coming?*

"Who is it?" Kaeja asked.

"It's Kyree."

"You knew he was coming?" she asked.

"No." Thank God I was already dressed and so was Kaeja.

He knocked again, and I stood there, blinking. I was trying to figure out why he thought popping up was better than texting.

"Are you going to open the door?" she asked with a frown, wondering why I was standing there like that.

"Oh, yeah. I am. I don't know if I should be pissed that Kyree popped his ass up over here or what."

"Well, let's see what he got to say."

I opened the door, and he removed his shades. When his eyes met mine, my heart skipped a beat.

"Good afternoon," he said. "I hope I'm not disturbing you. Damn, I didn't think your sexy ass could look sexier than yesterday, but I was wrong."

I blushed. "Thanks, but it's just some joggers. Come in."

"Just because you're dressed down doesn't make you less sexy." He walked in. As soon as he was inside, I closed the door.

"Hello," Kaeja greeted him.

"Hi," he said. "You must be Kaeja."

"Yeah. It's nice to meet you, Kyree."

She shook his hand, and I smiled so big. I was trying my best to contain my smile, but I couldn't help it. Kyree did that to me.

"I don't mean to pop up at your spot like this," he said. "It's not like me at all to pop up, but have you seen my phone? I can't find it anywhere, so I couldn't text you."

"No, I haven't seen it. That makes sense as to why you haven't responded to my texts. I've been texting you."

"I had a feeling you did. I have no idea what happened to my phone. I looked all over in my car and everything. I can't find it for nothing. You sure I didn't leave it here?"

"No, I remember you left with it in your hand because your cousin called," I said.

"Damn, that's right, I did. I hope I didn't drop it outside somewhere. I gotta buy a new one. Fuck."

"I've never lost my phone but these phones ain't cheap to go replace."

"It's not that bad," he chuckled. "It was time for an upgrade anyway."

"Have a seat," Kaeja said.

He sat down on the couch, and I sat next to him.

"What were you up to before I popped up?" he asked.

"I was doing a few sketches," I answered.

"I'm gonna leave you two alone and go to my room to catch up on my shows that I missed this week. It was nice meeting you," Kaeja said.

"It was nice meeting you too," Kyree replied.

Once Kaeja was in her room, she closed the door.

His cologne smelled so good, and it was invading my nostrils. I scooted closer, and he put his arm around my shoulder.

"I'm sorry I missed your calls and texts," he said.

"It's okay. I'm glad you came over. Kaeja told me that she'll be moving out with Avian soon."

Kyree studied my eyes. "How you feeling about that?"

"It makes me sad because I really am going to miss her. We've been roommates for the past five years, and it's like I need her to be here with me."

"The only thing you need is me," he replied with a serious tone.

I looked at him to see what exactly he meant by that. We'd just met and were still getting to know one another. "Oh, yeah?" I asked with a slight smile.

"Yeah. Am I interrupting your work? I can come back later," he said, looking over at my design table.

"No, you're good."

"You want to go with me to buy a new cell phone, so I won't have to miss any of your calls again?"

"Okay. Let me change and I'll be ready."

"All right. You don't have to get real fancy or nothing. We're going down the street to AT&T. Then we'll come back here and chill."

"Sounds good to me." I stood up.

Before I could go to my bedroom, he stood up, stepped in front of me, and placed both hands on my face. He planted a kiss on my lips. "I couldn't wait to do that again. I thought about you all night. Now go get dressed."

I hurried to my room, threw off my sweats, and put on a pair of jeans and a pink tank top. Right as I was putting on my sweater, Kyree walked into my bedroom.

"This is where you sleep?"

"Yeah," I replied, looking up. He'd startled me a little, but I didn't show it.

He nodded as he watched me put on my shoes. I grabbed my purse, and I looked in the mirror to make sure my hair was on point. He followed me out of the apartment. Kyree opened the door for me to get into his black Camaro. I watched him walk around to the driver's side as I applied my lip gloss.

He got the newest upgrade of his iPhone and paid $800 without any complaints. I had yet to upgrade mine because I couldn't afford it. iPhone released new phones before I was done paying the installments on my last phone. It was ridiculous to me. Kyree didn't like the installment plan, so he bought the phone upfront. Truth be told, it wasn't his money and his fancy clothes that impressed me. It was the way he looked at me that got to me. Those damn eyes.

When we got back to my apartment, he made sure all his contacts had been backed up.

"Well, at least I know now that you weren't ignoring me."

"I would never ignore you, so let's get that clear right now." He wrapped his arms around me and stared into my eyes. I took a deep breath as my heart started racing. I felt like I was in a dream. I felt like pinching myself to make sure this shit was real because it felt unreal. It had only been two days, and I was feeling all mushy inside.

"What do you think about me so far?" he asked.

"You're sweet. I like you."

"I like you too. Matter of fact, I would love to take you on a few dates. Is that cool?"

I grinned. "You want to date, date?"

"Yeah, don't you?"

"That will be fun. Will this be an exclusive dating thing, or are we dating others?"

"I would hope it's exclusive," he said, "unless you're seeing someone else, but I'm telling you right now, I'm a stingy muthafucka. I don't like to share."

"What's the first date?"

"I'll think of something," he replied. "Listen, Soraya, we just met. I don't want to come off sounding crazy, but I want you to myself, and you should have me to yourself. But we can do this however you want to do it. Don't let me pressure you."

"I don't feel pressured."

I wanted him to be all mine, but I didn't want to rush into this. I was excited, but there was something that I had been worried about. What about his son? I didn't have experience with dating anyone with kids. How involved would he want me to be?

"Would you want me to meet your son one day?" I questioned.

"There's no rush, because that will come in time. I don't want to rush anything else. We've done enough rushing."

I tried to hold my smile, but I couldn't. "Very true. We can go slow."

"Slow and steady but not too slow. You have the most beautiful smile. I swear, I think that's why I feel the way I do. I can't stop thinking about your smile," he said.

My heart melted like an ice cream cone on a hot Sunday afternoon. I put my arms around his neck and kissed his lips. I led him to my bedroom and closed the door. We wasted no time taking off all our clothes. Our passion was like one big ball of combustion ready to explode if held in any longer. Once I put that condom on him, I pushed him onto the bed and straddled him. I was grinding and rolling my hips, and he felt too good.

"Damn, baby, don't stop," he begged breathlessly, thrusting his hips up toward me.

I wasn't sure if it was possible to feel this way, but the way he was looking up at me, it was like I could see the love in his eyes. This juicy pussy was blowing his mind.

"Mmm-hmm," he hummed every time my dripping wet cave came down on him.

I closed my eyes tight as he started lightly kissing my breasts. My body started jerking, and although I didn't want to, I was going to explode.

"Not yet," he ordered. He pulled out of me and lifted me up at the same time. He flipped me on my back before getting right back inside of my warm center. "Damn, this shit is too damn good, baby."

"Yessss," I cooed knowingly.

"I'm going deep and you taking that shit like a champ."

He was hitting my deepest spot, and I was taking all of it. I even put my hands on his ass to pull him in deeper.

"Fuck!" he exhaled in an airy breath.

There was no need to let out all the freaky shit I liked to do all at once. If he were serious about being in an exclusive relationship, I would pull out all my tricks.

Kyree pulled me over the edge of the bed and moved me to get into the doggie-style position. He stood on the floor, and I tooted my ass up in the air. He reentered my pussy, and I moaned. I was allowing my inner bad girl to surface. It wasn't on purpose, and I swore that I was going to hold back, but I went with the flow.

"Damn, baby, I can't take it anymore," he said. "Come with me."

"I'm already coming."

"Let's come together then."

I had never before had an orgasm at the same time as a man, but I was on the brink of my orgasm. I moaned loudly enough for Kaeja to hear me. This would be payback for all the nights I had to listen to her and Avian.

As we were focusing on releasing together, his cell phone rang loudly.

"Damn, I thought I turned it off," he mumbled.

"Don't stop," I said, backing my ass up against him hard. I was ready to bust.

He ignored the ringing, and it stopped, but then it rang again. "Ahh, shit. Let me see who this is."

He stopped, and I turned over on my back as I tried to catch my quickened breath. As he checked his phone, I spread my legs and started playing with myself. He couldn't even fully concentrate on who it was as he stared at me.

"Damn!" He shut the phone off. "Fuck that phone. You look sexy as fuck right now."

He got on top of me so we could fuck some more. We didn't come once, we came multiple times, and it was the best sex of my life.

Chapter 13

Kyree

As I walked through the front door, India came down the hall with her hand over her chest. "You scared me half to death. I wish you would let me know when you're coming home."

It was close to two in the morning, and usually by now, she was asleep. "What's up?" I asked, taking a good look at her. She had the nerve to look surprised when I walked into my house. "Where's Kai?"

"In his bedroom, sleeping."

She didn't look well at all. She looked as if she had been crying, and her hair was all over her head. I'd turned my phone back on when I drove home and listened to the five voice messages of her crying. I was so sick of this shit and ready for her to move on with her life.

"I've been sick all day." She looked at me nervously. "So, um, I took a home pregnancy test. I don't want to hide this from you, but I'm pregnant, Kyree."

What did she say to me? Pregnant? I hadn't touched her in two months, so what was she talking about? I sighed because we never wore condoms when we had sex, but she was good about her birth control, so how did this happen? *Fuck!* Her news couldn't have come at a worse time. I was starting things with Soraya, and I didn't want to mess this up with her. I was going to be Soraya's man, but now this shit with India was going to fuck it all up.

"You keeping it?" I asked.

"Of course I am."

"Man, I'm not in the mood for this shit. We ain't even together and you thinkin' about keeping it? Anything to hold a nigga, huh?"

"You put your dick in me and created this baby. Sorry to fuck up your program, but it is what it is."

"I'm out here doing my thing. I met someone, and I'm dating her."

Her chest started heaving up and down. "You're dating her? Already?"

"Ay, stop thinking this shit between us is going to work out. It ain't!"

India scowled. "You will always be my man, and I will always be your woman. Since we were eighteen years old, that's what it's been. We have a five-year-old son, and we have a baby on the way now. Doesn't that make you want to cut this shit out? I mean, damn, for once can I be the only one?"

"No," I answered simply, without hesitation. Why would I do anything differently now because she was pregnant? India and I never had the same connection that Soraya and I had. I never considered India to be the one. This was something that she already knew, though.

"Oh, I get it," she said. "You must've gotten you some pussy tonight, huh? You think I don't know you, Kyree? You think that I don't know when a new bitch got your nose wide open? How much money does she have? Is she a doctor? Lawyer? Entrepreneur? That bitch will be in the wind as soon as she finds out that you about to suck the fucking life out of her. Hmmm, I may need to give her a heads-up."

Anger propelled through me as I answered, "She already knows about you, India. She even knows about Kai. I swear to God if you come at her and sabotage this,

I'll never talk to you again. You might as well get the fuck out right now!"

India instantly cried, "Seriously? It's barely two in the morning! You're so fuckin' evil! To think that I put up with all your shit for six years. To think I was down for you taking these broads' money and flossin' to provide for us. I sacrificed so much for you! My mama is right. I'm a fucking idiot."

"You can go live with your mama!"

"Fuck you, Kyree! You already know I'm not doing that."

I closed my eyes and took a deep breath. I didn't have to go there. I knew she couldn't stand her alcoholic stepfather. "I'm sorry, India. I didn't mean that. Listen, the last thing I want to do is to keep hurting you. Why force this when we know it's not working?"

"It's not working because you don't want it to work."

"I will always have some love for you, but I don't love you the way you want me to. I never could," I answered. "As the father of our children, I will always provide. You don't have to worry about that."

"You know what? This is what I'm going to do. I'm going to find me a real man to treat me right. I bet you would love that shit."

A text message from Soraya came through my phone before I could reply.

Soraya: I hope you made it home safe.

The way my face lit up when I texted Soraya back made India fold her arms across her chest. She never saw me fall in love with anyone, not even her. Women used to be all about business. My heart was never invested. The fact that I was falling in love with another woman rocked her to her core.

"Is that her?" she snapped as she clutched her stomach.

I looked at her as if she were crazy. "Good night, India."

"Give me the fucking phone, Kyree!" She charged at me.

"The hell you doing?" I snatched away and pushed her back, turning to walk to the bedroom.

She ran up on me and grabbed my arm, whipping me around forcefully. "Give me the phone right now! Let me tell that bitch that you're a no-good, lyin'-ass dog!" she yelled while swiping at the phone.

"Quit!"

When I didn't let her get her hands on it, she said, "Where you think the other phone disappeared to? I got rid of that one, and I'll get rid of this one too, bitch!"

I managed to hold the phone up in the air. I was too tall for her to reach my hands. There was no way she was going to get it.

I shook my head. "I figured you did some whack-ass shit like that. Stop!"

India glared at me through narrowed eyes as her tears flowed, and her nostrils were flaring. I put her through shit, but for whatever reason, she couldn't let me go. That she was pregnant again got under my skin because I had a feeling at that moment that she purposely stopped taking her birth control. The even more fucked-up part was that she was never going to let me go. She was afraid to love another man, and she was scared to lose me to another woman.

I went into the walk-in closet to change my clothes.

"Why can't you tell me why you don't love me, Kyree?" she cried.

I turned to look at her. "Because that would only fuck with your mind. Look, as long as you're here, don't ask why. I won't put her in your face, and I won't talk to you about her."

Her whole body shook as she fell to her knees. I would be a liar if I said that I felt good about hearing her crying so hard like that. It hurt to know that I hurt her. The more India cried, the worse I felt.

"Damn, look, stop crying like this." I cradled India in my arms, and her tears really started falling from her. "I don't want to hurt you."

"Kyree," she sobbed, "I thought what we had was so perfect, but I guess I made that all up in my mind. I can deal with you fucking other bitches for some dough, but falling in love is supposed to be off-limits."

"Lie down, India. I don't want you stressing over something you can't control. You're pregnant, and you need to relax. I didn't plan for none of this shit. I really didn't. You and I were never meant to be together, but that doesn't mean that I don't still care."

As she strolled back into the living room, she was making me feel bad. We'd agreed we were done. I didn't want to play games with her. India was hurting, and she wanted me to make her feel better. I walked into the living room and stared at her.

"You gonna be with her now?" India asked through clenched teeth as if she couldn't stand the thought to go through this.

I didn't answer as I stuck my hands in the pockets of my jeans.

"Answer me!" India demanded.

"I can't do this. I'm sorry. I'm sorry about everything, India, but you need to be out of here. You have three days." I went back into my closet to change.

India shouted, "I hate you!"

I put my clothes in the hamper and went to bed in my boxers.

India cried all night long. I put the pillow over my head, but it didn't drown out her crying. I'd never felt guilty or bad before, but that night, India made me feel like a piece of shit.

Chapter 14

Kaeja

A week passed, and throughout the days, I couldn't stop thinking about when Avian would finally give me the green light to move in. Without an exact move-in date, I felt he was slipping away from me, and the thought of us never living together consumed me. Between my selling homes and him being busy with his industry stuff, we weren't talking as much even though we made up. Not to mention, Soraya had Kyree over every single night. I now understood what it was like to hear sex sounds. I couldn't get any sleep, and it made me realize how insensitive I had been.

I needed to do something to fix my relationship with Avian. Since he hadn't given me a date, I decided to go ahead and move in. To be fair, I settled on leaving my bed. I was nervous about the thought of surprising him with a moving truck because I didn't know how he would react, but why couldn't we live together right now? What was the holdup? We could finally live together like we always talked about. I could've waited for him to give me a date, but fuck that, this was now or never! I didn't tell Soraya that Avian hadn't said yes because I didn't want her to talk me out of it. I called U-Haul for a truck and packed my things.

I knocked on Soraya's bedroom door, and she opened it.

"Hey, my truck is here. Can you guys help me?" I asked.

"Oh, you moving today?" Soraya looked surprised.

"Yeah, but I want to keep my big furniture here in case we try to kill one another," I said. "I'm even leaving my bed. If things work out, I'll arrange to have those things taken out."

"No problem. Kyree, let's help Kae with her stuff."

"Yeah, no problem." He stood up from the bed, and I directed them to the boxes in my bedroom.

When I pulled up to the curb of Avian's beach house, I could see him looking down at me from his window. I told him I was on my way, but I didn't say with a moving truck. He instantly came down the stairs in a white tank, gray Jordan sweatpants, and black Nike slides.

Avian blinked at me and stared as if I had lost my mind. "What is all this?"

"I'm moving in today, Avian," I declared as I got out of the truck. "Surprise!"

He folded his arms across his chest and replied, "This is what we're doing now? You think you can move in without talking to me about it first?"

Disappointment twisted at my heart because I was hoping that he would be as excited as I was. I swallowed the hard lump that had formed in my throat. "We always talk about moving in together one day, so I don't see what the big deal is. What would it matter if it's today or in a few months? It's time, or I'm done."

He sighed, walked briskly to the truck, and unfastened the hatch to pull the door. He lifted the gate and snatched a box from the back.

"Hey, be careful. My picture frames are in that box."

Ignoring me, he continued to walk up the stairs. I swore that if he broke my frames, he was going to be buying me some new ones.

Thankfully, I didn't have much in the back of that truck. I took a deep breath and took a box. We moved my things in complete silence. I stacked it all against his wall in the living room. Flopping down on the couch, I was exhausted and sweaty. He turned on the ceiling fan above me.

"I have to figure out where to put all your stuff," he complained as he went into the kitchen for two bottles of water. He came back in the living room with one for me and one for him.

"Thanks," I said. "It's not that much, just my clothes mostly."

He grunted before he asked, "Why do you have to always do shit on your time?"

I sipped the water and fired back, "My time? Seems like we've been doing everything on your time, Avian. We've been together for thirteen long-ass years. You don't think you're ready yet? If it's like that, then I'll take my stuff and we're done."

"No. No, forget it. I'm going to figure out where to put your stuff." He walked down the hallway to the back of the house. I could hear him in his closet, sliding his hangers around loudly.

I had upset him, but I was glad he didn't tell me to leave. I was bummed that he wasn't happy with my surprise, but at least we were going to live together now. Tears welled up as I started feeling wrong about forcing this on him. I fought my tears as I walked to the window and stared out at the beach. I loved Venice Beach. A few joggers and skateboarders cruised on the paved walkways.

"Kaeja," Avian called from the bedroom.

"Yeah?"

"Come here," he demanded.

I walked to his bedroom. "What's up?"

"When is Soraya's fashion show?" he asked from inside of the closet.

I went to the entry of the closet. "Next weekend. Why?"

"I wanted to make sure I didn't have anything else going on. This is Soraya's first show, and I want to be supportive."

"Well, that's sweet of you, baby. Does this mean you aren't mad at me anymore?"

"I'm not mad. I'm frustrated because you're giving me this ultimatum as if I don't love you. Baby, listen to me. This is not the way to fix us. We've been having issues lately, but you really should've confirmed this with me beforehand. I have to move some of these clothes to the other closet in the hall."

"I'm sorry, babe. I really want to spend every day with you. Why is that so hard for you to understand?" I burst into tears.

He stopped pulling clothes off the rack, and he stood in front of me. "Shhhh, don't cry. I'm swamped with work and stuff, so forgive me for being unattached. I want you to know that we can make this work. I have a terrible time with change, but we'll be okay."

I nodded, but I could tell when Avian wasn't honest about his feelings. I was terrified that I had made the biggest mistake ever.

Chapter 15

Kyree

India still hadn't moved, and it had been three days, but I couldn't handle putting her and my son out on the street, so I just refused to be there when she was. I enjoyed sleeping at Soraya's. Plus she didn't want to be alone since Kaeja had moved out. I went with India to a doctor's appointment that afternoon to confirm the pregnancy. I didn't want her lying to me about being pregnant to fuck with my head. As she said, she was pregnant, so I promised that I would be at every single appointment like I had with Kai.

Fendi sent me a text as I was leaving her appointment, wanting to hang.

Me: I'm doing right by Soraya, so if it involves women, I can't.

Fendi: Say less, my nigga. We'll get up soon.

Hanging with Fendi only brought unnecessary drama. It wasn't so bad being committed to one woman who had all the qualities I loved.

When I returned from India's doctor's appointment, I took Soraya shopping. Contrary to what India thought, I spent my own money how I wanted and when I wanted. Soraya picked out dresses, shoes, handbags, and I didn't care how much it cost. I wore high-end shit, so my woman was going to wear it as well. As soon as we were done shopping on Rodeo Drive and having sushi and cocktails at Katsuya Hollywood, we took the shopping bags to her place.

Soraya said, "I can't wipe this smile off my face."

"Good. Seeing your face light up was everything. Trust me, baby, this is only the beginning," I replied as I sat on her couch.

"Well, I love this beginning."

"Good, 'cause I want to be able to give you things that a man has never given you before."

"Awww, baby, that's so sweet," she cooed as she snuggled up with me. "I'm getting anxious about my first fashion show tomorrow. I hope everyone comes. Thank you so much for finding the venue and promoting it."

"Of course, it's what I do. No need to thank me. I want the absolute best for you."

"I want you to meet my mom," she said unexpectedly.

I smiled because that was a big step. Asking a nigga to meet her mom had to mean she wanted to take our relationship to that level. "I'd be honored, boo."

She looked up into my eyes. "You make me feel so special and loved. You keep it so real with me."

I lifted her chin and did my best to convince her, "I will be real with you. With me, there are no secrets. None. You can trust me to love you."

I could be real even when I knew I wasn't honest about my situation. I wanted to come clean, but I didn't know how. A part of me instantly felt guilty for letting that lie roll off my tongue that way, but I wanted her to trust me the way I trusted her.

She stood up in front of me and took off her shirt while looking deeply into my eyes. I loved it when she looked at me that way. She looked at me as if she would be mine for a lifetime. Yeah, I loved that shit. It didn't matter how many other brothers were before me, and it didn't matter how many other women were before her. This felt like a brand-new situation. When I was with her, I never wanted to leave. She was mine now, and I wasn't letting her go.

I slid my hands down the sides of her body before removing her jeans and then her panties. I stood up and picked her up off her feet. While she giggled infectiously, I laid her on the couch and pressed my body on top of hers. With her pussy exposed, I positioned myself between her legs. I moved her legs to sit on my shoulders. Long licks of my tongue soon followed. I moaned and sent vibrations through her pussy. I sucked slowly, pulling her clit softly into my mouth. My tongue worked once I found my rhythm.

She screamed, "Oh, my God!" Gripping my head, clenching me tightly, she exploded like a fountain. "Kyree. Oh, Kyree!"

In the throes of passion, she started bucking toward the ceiling until her screams hit a high pitch. As soon as she was done, I came up for air and lay between her legs. I ran my fingers through her hair and stared at her.

"Why are you looking at me like that?" she asked through her heavy breathing. She was trying her best to recuperate.

"Because you are the most beautiful woman I have ever seen, Soraya."

"Oh, babe. Thank you," she replied as she ran her hand across my dick.

I undressed so she could please me. I loved it when she took control. She kissed my lips, my chin, my neck, and then moved down to my hardened flesh. Her tongue had massaged the tip before she pushed me all the way into her mouth. I closed my eyes and took a deep breath. With every lick, she made me feel so damned good. Shudders ran through my entire body, as she wasted no time in returning the favor. I exploded into her mouth. Instead of spitting me out, she swallowed every drop. Damn, I loved her.

After our lovemaking session, I realized that I had run out of clothes, and I needed to go home to get more. Soraya had some things to go over for the fashion show the following day, so I told her I would meet her after I went home real quick. I pulled up to my house and walked up to the door. When I put my key in and tried to turn it, it wouldn't unlock.

What the fuck? Did she fuck with my locks?

"India!" I hollered as I knocked on my front door. She was here, because her Toyota was in my driveway. I beat on that door until my hand hurt.

She finally opened the door, but only partly as the chain was attached. She spoke through the small opening as if she wasn't going to let me in. "What you want, Kyree?"

"What I want? Why you change my locks? This ain't even your damn house!"

"If it's your house, I sure can't tell. You're never even here. I thought you maybe you moved out and left the house to us."

"It's only been four days, India. I saw you this afternoon, and you didn't say shit about changing the locks."

"You didn't say shit about when you were coming home. Your son ain't seen you in four days, and you want to come up in here today? It doesn't work like that, playa."

I said in the calmest voice I could, "Let me in my house. You got me out here looking crazy as shit."

She closed the door. I could hear the chain being taken off. She opened the door and let me inside. As soon as I looked at her, I wanted to knock her ass out for playing games. She knew good and well that I hadn't moved out, because all my belongings were still here. Plus I would never leave her the house my grandmother's insurance money bought. She was lucky I didn't toss her ass out on the street.

I looked around, but nothing seemed out of place. I didn't see my son. "Where's Kai?"

India closed the door behind me and said, "Oh, so now you want to see him? He's with my mom. I needed a little break. I've been a little stressed out."

"Stressed out for what? What's goin' on? You look like shit."

"Humph, the nerve of you. You really don't get it, do you?"

I sat on the couch and shrugged. "What am I not getting?"

"You don't even sleep here anymore. It's like that, huh? We're over? Is that what you want to tell me?"

"India, what the fuck? We've been over! I thought you were gettin' it, but I see that you still misunderstanding what I want."

"Clearly, we have one big fuckin' misunderstanding, Kyree. I don't want you here, and you don't want to be here! How about you get out? Get the rest of your shit, 'cause I'm sure your new bitch would love to have you. Please find somewhere to park your raggedy cars before I sell them! Got them lined up along the curb, swearing your mechanic skills will get them running. Them shits haven't run in years."

"I'm not moving out of my house, and you're batshit crazy if you think I am! You get the fuck out! And you not gonna sell shit. If my cars move, watch."

"Watch me move that shit!"

"Whatever. You ain't gonna do shit. Why are you still here? Get the fuck out!"

"No, you get the fuck out! This is where my son and I are staying. You stay downtown off Wilshire with that bitch, remember?"

A chill ran through me. *Wait, what?* "How do you know where she lives?" I narrowed my eyes at her.

"Oh, what? You thought I wasn't going to find out where you been staying? You should turn off the location tracker when you post y'all li'l pictures on Facebook, playa. I swear you're so fuckin' stupid!"

"I'm stupid? You shouldn't throw stones when you live in a glass house, baby."

"So I'm stupid?"

"If the shoe fits . . ."

"I can't believe you!" she erupted. "You made me fall for your charm and all your lies. You made it seem like we would always be together and that nothing would ever break our bond. You promised to never hurt me. Now you're telling me that all that goes out the window because she sucks you and fucks you better than I do? You know what? You're right. I am stupid. I'm stupid for loving you! Ugh, I can't stand your lying ass!"

"What I lie to you about? We agreed that we were done, and I've always kept it real, even when I wasn't feeling you."

"Yeah, right. You tell half-truths all the time. How about you tell her about how many women you've conned out of money, how many have had abortions, and how you and Fendi went to prison for stealing a bitch's Ferrari and her checkbook? Soon she'll be pregnant, you'll get tired of her, and she'll be in my shoes. By that time, I will be long gone. Trust me, Ky. I'm so done with you."

"If I'm all those things, why you still want me then?"

She paused before she said, "I'm too invested and clearly retarded."

"Whatever! I'm having the locks changed, and you will not have a key. Since your name ain't on any mortgage papers, if you don't get out soon, I'll have the police remove you. And you leave my son here. Until you get a place, he's not going with you."

She stared at me with her head cocked to the side. "Get what you came here to get and get the fuck out!"

I took a deep breath and blew out stifling air while I called the locksmith. Why couldn't she make this easy for me? I was ready to bring Soraya to see my home, but I couldn't do that if India was here making my life a living hell.

Chapter 16

Kaeja

I tried to fit into a dress to wear to Soraya's fashion show, but there was no way, and I did not have time to go shopping for something new to wear. Soraya made this dress for me, but she made it four months ago, and I couldn't fit into it. I hadn't noticed how much weight I'd put on. There was no time to have her adjust it, not when she was so busy preparing for her show.

"What you going to do?" Avian asked as he fixed his suit jacket in the mirror.

"I'm going to call her." I grabbed my cell phone off the dresser to call Soraya one more time. Hopefully, she had a dress at the house I could fit into. I had been trying to reach her all morning, but she wasn't answering. This time, she picked up but didn't speak.

"Raya?"

"Yeah," she said, sounding out of breath.

"Shit, it's about time you answered!"

"Girl, today is so hectic. This must be an emergency because you've called me a billion times."

"It is an emergency. I can't fit into the dress you made for me. I gained a little weight."

"You pregnant?"

"Hell no! I must have gained a little weight since I last tried on this dress a few months ago. Please say that you have a size ten floating around somewhere."

"One sec." She put me on hold. After a few moments of me crossing my fingers and praying she had something for me, she said, "I have a size ten at the house. You still have the key, right?"

"Yeah, I do. Thank you, girl. I love you. I didn't want to miss your event, and I don't want to be late."

"Awww, I love you, Kaeja. See you when you get here," she said.

I ended the call. Avian sighed heavily. He hated running late to anything, but he should've understood that I was having a crisis.

"All your commotion is starting to make me sweat," he said in a dry voice. His phone rang before I could tell him to shut up. He answered it. "Hello."

I looked for my sandals in the closet. I could hear a female's voice coming from the other end of his phone. I didn't look at him as I zeroed in on the conversation. It could've been someone from work or an artist he was working with, but I was still straining to hear.

"What's up?" he asked whoever that was in an awkward tone. "I'm heading out with Kaeja right now to Soraya's fashion show. I'll call you later." He turned his back to me.

Her voice got louder. This time, I could hear her clear as day. "Avian, I don't give a fuck about that bitch! Your ass is supposed to answer my calls whenever I call!"

"I'll call you back." He ended the call and cleared his throat.

I turned around to face him with a straight face, but I didn't say anything at first.

"You ready so I can take you to get this dress? I'm not trying to be later than we already are," he said.

"Who was that?"

"Nobody. Let's go."

Did he lie to my face?

I felt tears welling up in my eyes, and I was crying before I knew it. I wanted Avian to be my husband one day, but that day seemed like a stupid fantasy. In high school, we were head over heels for one another. He was my first love and my everything

"You're going to lie to my face?" I asked. "I heard her voice. Who was that?"

He took a deep breath and exhaled. "Let's go." Avian walked out of the room.

I couldn't find the right words to say because I was speechless at how he downplayed this. I'd heard her! I took a deep breath and thought about Soraya. This was her night. I would address this matter late, so I made sure that I had my purse and makeup so I could do my makeup in the car on the way.

When I locked the door to the house, he was already in the car with the engine revved up. I got in wearing a deep frown. My mind was racing a mile a minute, trying to figure out how was I going to be able to blast his ass for cheating on me. I fastened my seat belt in complete silence.

"Kaeja. You all right?" he asked, even though I was far from that.

I was about two seconds away from slapping the shit out of him. I couldn't believe what I had heard. Her voice was so loud and clear. This broad had the nerve to be bold enough to call me a bitch. The way she said it like she knew me, it had to be Lelee.

"I can't believe that you would do me like this," I said.

His phone was vibrating through his pocket. He drove down the street, heading toward Soraya's place as if his pocket weren't buzzing.

"Kaeja, I'm not doing you like anything."

"I swear, Avian . . . Please stop talking to me. Don't talk to me for the rest of the night!" I sat up straight and brushed back my tears.

Chapter 17

Soraya

Everyone in the building clapped for me as the show ended. I walked on the catwalk behind the models. I waved, feeling proud of my collection. Being in love had inspired some of my best work, and Paradise You had officially completed its very first collection. Cameras flashed, and the house was packed. I glanced over at Kyree as he whistled with two fingers in his mouth.

It was crazy how most of the night whizzed by so quickly. It was this adrenaline rush, and I loved it. I couldn't wait to do my next show. Kyree brought me long-stemmed white roses backstage.

"I'm so proud of you, baby. You did an excellent job. I'm sure every woman up in here will be trying to buy your pieces."

"Awww, thank you, babe."

He kissed my lips, and I took the roses from him. He was so reassuring and gentle with me when I felt like my designs weren't good enough. The support he showed surpassed what I expected from him, because we had only been together for a month and a half.

Avian and Kaeja came backstage, and even though she had a smile on her face, her eyes looked sad, and she wasn't standing close to Avian as she usually did. He tried to hold her hand, and she pulled away.

"You guys coming to the after-party?" I asked as soon as they reached me.

"Of course," Avian responded, giving Kaeja a smile. She rolled her eyes and didn't make eye contact with me.

"Thank you, guys, for coming," I said.

Kaeja said, "I'm your best friend. I will always support you."

"I know, but I still want to thank you. It means so much to me, and I never want to take that for granted."

I spotted Lelee and a few of her homegirls across the room. She was looking like a damned stalker watching Avian. I held my breath as she stood in front of Kaeja and Avian. She moved toward us so fast, I didn't have time to warn Kaeja.

"I thought I'd come over and say hello," Lelee said with a smile.

This was not the time or the place for a confrontation or a fight to erupt. Kaeja wasn't the confrontational type, but she also wasn't the type to back down from anybody.

"You can keep your hello, bitch, 'cause we're good over here," Kaeja said.

Lelee snickered. "Why don't you end this little game, Avian, and tell her what's really going on? I'm tired of being your little secret."

Before Avian could say a word, Kaeja let go of his arm and hit Lelee in the face. Lelee was fighting right back. They both were throwing and landing hard punches. Avian grabbed Kaeja, and Kyree managed to get Lelee out of Kaeja's reach.

"Bitch!" Kaeja shouted.

"Bitch!" Lelee shouted back. That was all everyone heard from their mouths as they were being separated.

Kaeja had pieces of Lelee's weave in her hands. She threw her hair on the ground and marched off in the opposite direction. Avian tried to follow her, but I pulled him back. This was his fault, and there was nothing he could say to fix it.

"I'll go get her, you piece of shit!" I shouted at him.

The crowd was dispersing, and everyone was leaving after that. I was glad the show had been over, but I hadn't had the chance to find out if anyone wanted to buy anything. A good ol' hood brawl had happened, and the rest of my event was ruined.

"Are you okay?" I asked Kaeja when I caught up with her at the back door of the venue.

She was crying hysterically. "Avian is cheating on me with that nasty bitch! I've been having these feelings, and now it's true."

I held her close to me as I hugged her. "Don't cry. It's okay. Fuck him! Move back in."

She cried harder.

Kyree came to the back. "Are you okay?"

"I'll be fine. Where's Avian?" Kaeja asked.

"He, um, went to check on that girl—"

"He did what?" Kaeja tried to break out of my arms, but I wouldn't let her go.

"Don't, Kae. cool off," I said.

"You don't want to make a bigger scene," Kyree said gently.

"I'm done with him! It's over!" Kaeja cried. "I won't put up with this shit. God knows how long it's been going on. I'm over here looking stupid."

"No, you're not," Kyree said. "You're in love, and when you're in love, you choose to see what you want to see. Trust me, give it a few days and then talk to him. It's better to talk when you're not mad."

"I don't want to speak to him ever again. I'm sorry, Raya. I'm sorry I messed up your night. I can't go to the after-party. Can I come home?"

"Girl, you don't have to ask. Your room will always be your room."

"Okay," Kaeja sobbed.

I rubbed her back and looked at Kyree. He nodded with understanding.

Chapter 18

Kaeja

Ding-dong.

Ding-dong.

Ding-dong.

The doorbell was ringing the next morning, and I wished I could've ripped out the wires to stop it. The first sensation that I felt when I opened my eyes was a pain. I was lying on my old bedroom floor with a bottle of Henny in my hand, and my head was pounding. I was hoping Soraya would answer the door, but I realized that she wasn't because the whole house was silent. I could hear the doorbell, and it was getting on my nerves. I got up from the floor, holding my pounding head.

The last thing I remembered was coming back to the apartment with Soraya and Kyree, but then they left to go to the after-party. I didn't mind being alone at first, but quickly, my sadness consumed me. I wanted to drink away my misery, and I cried myself to sleep. I didn't remember anything else. I looked at the clock on my way out of my bedroom to see that it was barely six in the morning.

The doorbell sounded again.

"Go away," I grumbled as I looked out of the peephole.

It was Avian, looking like a lost, sick puppy with his head down and hands in his sweatshirt's pockets. I wasn't in the mood to see his ass. Not this soon.

Soraya came out of her room in a T-shirt and no pants. "Who is that?" she asked through squinted eyes.

"Who else? Avian's dumb ass."

Soraya groaned, "I'm going back to bed."

I was hesitant because I didn't want to see his lying face, but then again, I wanted to hear his reasoning for cheating on me. As soon as I opened the door, I wished I hadn't, because the sight of him made me want to bust his head wide open. The sunlight came in without warning and caused my head to thump even harder. I put my hand up to shield the sun from my eyes.

"What do you want?"

"Kaeja, I'm sorry—"

I put my hand in his face so he could stop talking. The rest of what he wanted to say was going to be ignored. I turned away from him and flopped down on the couch. My eyes could barely focus, so I stopped trying and closed them. He came in and closed the door behind him.

"Are you still my baby?" he asked.

I turned my back to him and faced the couch. I didn't want to look at him at all. I didn't even want to be near him. He made me sicker to my stomach. If he had told me what was going on, that whole incident would've been avoided. Lelee deserved to have her ass kicked, yes, but I wouldn't have chosen that moment to do it.

"Why didn't you tell me about Lelee? Do you love her?" I kept my eyes on the couch. Tears came to my eyes. Deep down, he loved me, but I had to ask anyway. I needed to understand why he screwed up this way.

Silence blanketed the living room, as Avian said nothing.

"Do you love her, Avian?" I asked again with force behind my voice.

"Of course not," he sighed heavily.

"Why didn't you tell me that you were fucking her at least?" I curled up into a ball, and I couldn't stop myself from crying so hard. I was crushed, and my heart was shattered into a billion pieces.

Avian came to me, and he stroked my back. He stroked my hair, and I didn't protest. There was something about his touch that made me feel like everything was going to be all right, but I realized I wasn't the type of woman to be weak.

"Get out, Avian. Leave. I will make sure I get everything from your house this week."

He didn't try to talk me out of it. He didn't even say a single word. Why couldn't he answer any of my questions about Lelee? I deserved at least that much. He walked out of the apartment and closed the door behind him gently.

I wished I'd never opened that door, because now I felt even worse. His guilt and his unresponsiveness created this pain in the deepest part of my soul. I felt broken.

Chapter 19

Kyree

As soon as Soraya had gotten up to see who was at the door, she was back in bed and in my arms. The after-party the night before was popping. We had fun celebrating her new collection. We danced, we drank, and then we came home and had some of the wildest sex. We had already been up talking before the doorbell rang.

"Okay, so back to what we were talking about," she said.

"Who was at the door?" I asked.

"Avian. Kaeja answered it. Looks like he's here to plead his case."

"I bet."

"Anyway, one of my fantasies is to have a threesome with another woman," she said.

"For real? Have you ever been with a woman?"

"No, but I think it's sexy for two women to share one man."

"It can be, but I don't think you would be able to handle another woman doing what you do to your man. I've been in that position before, but I never want to share you with another woman. You'll never have to worry about me asking you to do it either. What we have is between us and nobody else."

My cell phone was ringing, but I ignored it.

"You should answer that. It might be your son," Soraya said with a genuine smile as she walked over to the bathroom and closed the door.

I'd told her that India had been keeping him from me, but I didn't say it was because I kicked her out.

I missed the call, but a text followed.

India: I'm in the hospital. I lost the baby.

I eased out of bed with a groan. "Hey, uh, baby," I said through the bathroom door, "I gotta go. There's an emergency I need to get to."

I texted India to let her know I was on my way. She texted me back with the room number.

The toilet flushed. "Oh, no. Is it your son?" Soraya said. She washed her hands and came out of the bathroom. "Is he all right?"

"I don't know." I went with it because I didn't want to explain. "I have to go check on him." I placed a kiss on her forehead before finding something to wear quickly. "I'll keep you posted." I threw on some jeans and a black T-shirt with my black and gold Giuseppe Zanottis. "I'll call you as soon as I find out what's going on with him, okay?"

"Okay. I'm going back to sleep. I'll see you when you get back."

She kissed my lips. I grabbed my keys and jetted out of the door.

As soon as I got to the hospital, I had to figure out what room India was in. I was in such disarray that I couldn't focus on where my phone was, and I didn't know what room India was in without it. I had a flashback of tossing the phone back on the bed. "Shit," I said to myself. I didn't feel like going back to Soraya's to get it.

I stopped at the gift shop for some flowers. After getting her room number from the information desk, I went up the elevator.

I stepped into her room. Her mother was there, and Kai had his head in her lap, sleeping. Sheila was the dark-skinned version of India and was young enough to be her sister because she'd had her when she was 15. I took a deep breath and exhaled. Shelia was the last person I wanted to see right now. I placed the flowers on the table beside India's bed.

India's mother went in on me. "How dare you come up in here like you care? You put my daughter and her son out on the street, causing her to have a miscarriage."

I was so tired of India involving her mother in our shit. I wasn't in the mood. This wasn't about her, and this wasn't any of her business. "I do care," I objected. "You have no idea what's going on, so stay out of it."

India's mom started to say something but stopped once she saw India sit up in the bed.

"Hey, how are you doing?" I asked India.

"I lost our daughter while your ass was lying up with the next bitch. What do you mean, how am I doing? Clearly stressed the fuck out, and it's all your fault."

"How you know it was a girl? You're not even three months pregnant."

"Get out!" she screamed.

I refused to leave, because it didn't matter if I didn't want to be with her. I wasn't that cold-blooded.

"Did you hear my daughter? She said get out!"

Kai lifted his head from his grandmother's lap and sat up on the couch. As soon as he saw me, he stood up and came to me. I hugged him. "Hey, son."

"Hi, Dad," he replied. This wasn't the time or the place to do this in front of our 5-year-old.

"No disrespect, but I'm not leaving."

"You keep treating my daughter like this, Kyree. You would never think that the two of you are married acting this way. Neither one of you wears your damn wedding rings."

I wanted to go off, but I wasn't going to, not in front of my son. I had put India through enough. I had taken off my ring only a few months after marriage, but India had only recently stopped wearing hers. I never considered us to be married because it was over as soon as we said I do.

Chapter 20

Soraya

I ran the shower water hot, the way I liked it. As I looked in my closet for something to wear, I heard my phone ding. I looked at it on the end table and realized it wasn't my phone. I heard it again, coming from the bed. Kyree's phone was lying right there, and I couldn't call him to tell him that it was here. I thought about leaving it there, but it dinged again like whoever it was had a lot to say. I picked it up, but I couldn't see any of the texts. I had watched him enter his code so many times I knew it.

"Don't look, Raya," I said aloud.

I put it on the end table and started to walk to the bathroom, but it dinged again. Biting my lower lip, I turned around and picked his phone back up. My heart was racing as I thought that I would be crazy as hell to go through his phone. I stopped because I always believed that when you went looking for stuff, you got more than what you were looking for. I put his phone down and sat on the edge of the bed. My stomach was swirling, telling me something was going on, but then again, if it were nothing, then I would have nothing to worry about. I hopped off the bed, picked up the phone, and entered his code. His phone unlocked, and I had access.

I pushed the text icon to see that the last few messages were from someone confirming an event. I should've put the phone down at that point, but I noticed there were a few from India. I clicked on it. My eyes started to water as I read about her being at the hospital because she lost their baby. My heart plummeted into my stomach as I scrolled up to see if there were any other messages between them, but there weren't any. So she was pregnant, and she lost the baby. What kind of man left a woman when she was pregnant with her second child? I quickly wiped my tears. I didn't know what their full story was, but I wasn't going to wait for him to tell me. I had the hospital room number, and I was going to go up there to see for myself.

With my mind running so fast, I showered, got dressed, and was out the door. Kyree had some serious explaining to do. The more I thought about this situation, the angrier I got. This was fucked up for real. Kyree rushed up out of my bed to be at her side, and that confused me. Were they still together? I wasn't about to sit in this house and drive myself crazy trying to figure it out.

Chapter 21

Kyree

"This marriage was over before it started, Mama, so I'm not wearing that ring. I don't claim him as my husband because he doesn't deserve that title," India said. "He's a liar and a cheater!"

India's mother rolled her eyes in disgust. "I don't understand it. You call me talking about y'all broke up. You can't break up when you're married, India. You knew he was a cheater, but you married the no-good dog anyway."

"Hey, I'm not trying to disrespect you, Sheila, but stay out of my business," I said.

"Too late, 'cause I'm all up in it. What you gon' do?" Her eyes were nearly bucking out of her head as she stared me down.

Suddenly, the hospital door opened, and Soraya walked inside. I stood there speechless while India and her mother looked at her like she was crazy.

"Excuse me," Soraya said. "I don't mean to interrupt, but Kyree, you forgot your phone." She handed it to me with a wildfire blazing in her eyes. Oh, she looked pissed the fuck off. I was in deep shit. *Wait, how did she read my text messages?* I had a lock code on it.

India snapped rudely, "Who the fuck are you?"

Soraya briefly looked at her before she looked at Kai, and then back at me. "I'm glad to see that your son is okay."

Before I could find the right words to say, she walked out of the room.

"Was that her?" India's mother asked.

"Yeah, that was his li'l bitch, Mama." She looked at me. "Nigga, you don't even know how to be real with nobody. Your dumb ass left your phone at her house and didn't make sure you had it before coming here. So sloppy."

I heard her, but I was trying to figure out how I was going to fix things. I thought about bolting out after her or calling her as soon as I left, but I wondered if that would be enough.

"You have managed to make a fool of me for the last time. All this stress caused me to lose our child, but you know what? I'm over it!"

"Then get a divorce, India, since you're done," Sheila spat. "I'll help you file if that's the problem."

"Don't worry about it, 'cause I'll file," I said.

India replied, "Good, 'cause I can't do this anymore. I got a few more things I need to get from the house, and then you'll never have to see me again."

"I'll bring your things to your mother's house," I said. "Oh, but wait, she can't come over there, huh, Sheila? Why you let your alcoholic-ass husband dictate your life? He won't even let your daughter and your grandson stay with you."

Sheila shouted, "Oh, hell no! You don't worry about what goes on in my house. She's coming to get her shit so she can be done with ya tired ass! You ain't been nothin' but trouble from the moment you two got together. Good fucking riddance."

I sucked my teeth and swatted my hand her way as if she were an irritating fly.

"Mama, I bet that she doesn't even know we're married," India said.

I jumped in before Sheila could respond. "You said it yourself that our marriage was over before it started. Don't worry about what she knows and what she doesn't. Call me when you're ready to come to get your shit."

I kissed the top of my son's head. "I'll see you later, man. Okay?"

He nodded. "Bye, Daddy."

"Bye, son."

I walked out of the room and made my way to the elevator. I couldn't stop thinking about how hurt Soraya looked when she entered the room. I fucked up, and I should've kept it one hundred with her from the start. Once the elevator reached ground level, I got out and walked to exit the hospital.

To my surprise, Soraya was pacing back and forth in the lobby near the exit doors. Was she waiting for me?

Chapter 22

Soraya

I wanted to talk to Kyree face-to-face to find out exactly what was going on, so that was why I waited around. I didn't have to wait long because he was approaching me after only a few minutes. It was like I couldn't leave without hearing what he had to say. I didn't think he would come down so quickly, but I was willing to wait for him so we could talk.

It wasn't like me to go through anyone's phone, but there was something about the way he left that I couldn't put my finger on. I watched him put his passcode in his phone so many times that I was able to get right into his phone. Reading her text messages to him hurt like hell.

I paced back and forth, unable to figure out what I was going to say to him. I was confused and hurt. I felt like we had gotten to the point where we could talk about everything, so I didn't understand why he didn't tell me everything.

"Soraya, it's not what you think," he started to explain as I looked up to see him walking toward me.

"Oh, so she didn't lose your baby?"

"No, um, well yeah, she did, but—"

"So it is what I'm thinking then. You lied and said that your son had an emergency. You never mentioned that she was pregnant again. Are you still with her, Kyree? Is that what's going on?"

"No! India and I had been broken up a little over a month before I met you. Then she found out she was pregnant a few weeks ago and decided to keep it. I'm sorry for not telling you as soon as I found out. I honestly don't know how I thought I was going to hide that from you, especially if she had the baby."

"God, this is the craziest shit ever! Is there anything else you want to tell me?"

"No. That's everything. Please tell me we're good, Soraya."

"Nah, we ain't good, nigga. Please don't come to my place." I walked away from him and out of the hospital. "We're done."

I was hurt and embarrassed. I missed Jacoury so much. I missed the way he used to make me laugh. Why did he ever have to go to jail?

I was angry at myself of moving so fast, living this fairy tale when he lied to me so quickly and effortlessly that it made me think that he could've been lying about everything else. I didn't know him well enough to tell when he was lying. How could I trust him and build a relationship? I thought Kyree was different, but the whole ordeal had me in a fucked-up mood.

As soon as I got home, I went into Kaeja's room to check on her. This wasn't the time to discuss my issues. I wanted to make sure my friend was all right. "Kaeja?" I asked as I knocked on her door.

"Come in," she said.

She was sitting on the edge of her bed, watching her feet dangle slowly. She looked up at me with her bloodshot eyes, and her hair was sticking straight up as if she had been electrocuted.

"I don't understand why he would cheat on me," she sobbed.

I sat down next to her on the bed. I hugged her, and she cried in my arms. I wished that she didn't have to feel so hurt. "It's going to be okay. It will take some time."

"Avian is all I know. How will I ever move on?"

"In time, you won't feel this hurt. All you need is time. I can't tell you how long to heal or deal with this. You guys spent thirteen years together. Plus you still have to get all of your things out of his apartment."

She moaned and groaned. "I'm dreading that part. I . . ." She cried hard, and she shook uncontrollably. I kept my arms around her. I let her have her cry on my shoulder. She needed to get it out.

Her phone beeped, and she picked it up from beside her. It was a text from Avian. She read his text aloud: "You doing all right?" She rolled her eyes and sucked her teeth.

A part of me wondered if Avian was even sorry for what he had done. Right when I was about to take her phone from her to shut it off, she powered it off.

"You don't need him bothering you. Get some rest. You need anything from the kitchen?" I asked as I stood up.

"I can't eat right now. I feel so sick."

"Okay, lie down, and I'll come to check on you in a bit. When you go back to work? I'm sure they miss you."

"The office has been calling to check in on me. I can't go to work feeling like this. I won't be able to concentrate."

"You want me to make you something to eat?"

"No."

"Kaeja, don't starve yourself. I'll check on you in a bit."

I closed the door and walked to my bedroom. As soon as I fell back on my bed, I picked up my cell. I pulled up my contacts and typed Jacoury's name. I thought about calling him. My finger lingered over his name, but then I stopped myself. What if his girlfriend was right there? It wouldn't be right to hit him up because my shit didn't work out. I tossed my phone next to me and grabbed the remote to turn on my TV.

Chapter 23

Kaeja

I spent the next fourteen days on stress leave from work, crying until my tears ran out. I bathed, did my hair, ate, went for a few walks, and I finally felt well enough to go to work. I had an open house for a client, and if I didn't get it together, I would have to pass this deal to one of my associates. I was grateful that the client wanted me to be the person to sell her house.

As far as Avian and I were concerned, we were done. I didn't have to worry about going to his house to get my things because he had them delivered by movers as if he couldn't wait to get my shit out of there. He had someone else pack up my shit and drop it off. I was livid, but Soraya had a good point when she said at least I didn't have to see his face again.

After showering, dressing, and doing my hair, I threw my shades over my eyes and closed the door to my bedroom behind me before leaving to head to an open house I'd scheduled. Soraya was in the kitchen, making breakfast.

"Look who's alive," Soraya joked. "I'm happy you feel good enough to get out of the house and go to work."

"Yeah, I had to take some time to get my mind together. I can't waste away in my bedroom any longer. Plus I could use the money right now. The good news is that I have an open house today."

"I'm sure you'll get an offer. You always do."

"Thanks. I've been so consumed with me that I meant to ask you about you and Kyree. I haven't seen him around lately, and you haven't even mentioned his name. What's up with that?"

"There's no need to bring him up. I am no longer seeing Kyree, but that is another story, so we need to have drinks."

"I feel like such a bad friend because you've been there for me and I was so busy being depressed that I hadn't noticed you were going through something too."

"Kae, I'm good. Trust me, but we will have drinks when you come home this evening. Okay?"

"Okay," I said. "Well, I hope you have a good day too."

"Thanks, girl. I'll see you later," she said.

"Bye." I walked out of the apartment and headed down the stairs.

I headed down the walkway to where my car was parked against the curb. As much as I hated driving the white Mercedes-Benz CLA 250 because it was a gift from Avian, I didn't have any other wheels to roll in. After thirteen years of being together without any real breaks, my life was feeling weird without him. I understood that no man was going to be perfect, but I couldn't tolerate disrespect. Thirteen years wasted, and I was simply trying to figure out how to put the pieces of my life back in order. That day was the first step I took toward finding happiness.

I backed out of the stall and headed to the grocery store. I always had cookies for my open house. Looking at the time, I realized that I needed to hurry up. I pulled up into the store's parking lot in no time because the store was down the street. I hopped out of my car, locked it, and briskly walked into the store.

As I walked over to the bakery section, I couldn't decide on chocolate chip or oatmeal raisin. I put the chocolate chip tray back, I grabbed the oatmeal, but then I put it back. I stood there, thinking about what kind most people liked.

"Tough decision?"

I jumped at the sound of a male's voice next to me. I turned to see a man with a familiar face, but I didn't recognize him right off.

His eyes were looking directly at me as he stood a few feet away. He made me feel uncomfortable for a minute, but once he smiled, he made me want to take off my shades to get a better look at him, but I didn't want him to think I was checking him out. I kept my shades on and tried my best to see who he was. His brown skin and perfect grin had my full attention.

The more I stared at him, the more I realized that I did know him. We went to high school together, but he was also an actor now. Soraya and I had seen him in one of his movies.

"Nate Townsend?" I asked, seeing if it really was him.

"Kaeja James. You remember me?" he replied, looking surprised.

"Of course I do. How you been?"

He brandished that handsome grin. "I'm good. How you doing?"

"I'm good these days. It's good to see you."

"Good to see you too. You still hang out with Soraya Pierce?"

I nodded with a smile. "I sure do. We're actually roommates."

"That's dope. How are your parents?"

"Um, they're good," I pretended to know. I hadn't talked to my parents in so long that I didn't know anything. I figured they were okay because I hadn't been called. "And yours?"

"Divorced, but good nonetheless."

"Sorry to hear that," I replied, remembering how lovely his parents had been the few times I saw them at the school on parents night.

"It was for the best. Sometimes people are better apart than together. You, uh, having a hard decision with those cookies?" he asked, coming a little closer but still keeping a comfortable distance.

"Yeah, I have an open house in about forty-five minutes, and I can't decide if I should get the chocolate chip or oatmeal raisin tray," I said.

He shook his head and laughed. It was a deep, cheerful, and light laugh as if he had no worries and no problems. "Real estate agent, I take it?"

"Yeah."

"That's great! You changed your mind about being a doctor."

"I realized while in medical school that I wouldn't be happy."

"I understand how that goes. You want my honest opinion on the cookies?" he asked with his hand on his chin.

"Sure."

"Not too many love oatmeal raisin cookies the way they love chocolate chip, but there are those who prefer oatmeal. I would get the assorted tray. There's both chocolate chip and oatmeal, but it includes peanut butter, which is my favorite."

"True. I didn't even think of doing that. Thank you for helping me." I picked up the assorted tray.

"It's all good. It was good to see you again." He smiled, reaching across me to grab a tray of peanut butter cookies. He put them in his basket. "I really don't need to eat all these, but I can't resist."

I got a whiff of his scent. He smelled fresh like citrus or something. Before I could think to do anything else, I took in how handsome he was. After being with Avian for all those years, it was nice to look at another man.

"Congrats on your acting endeavors," I said, not wanting to leave his presence yet. "You're terrific."

He smiled genuinely, showing off the sexiest pair of dimples I had ever seen. I didn't know he had dimples like that, but then again, I never looked that hard before. *Good Lord!* His dimples were deeper than mine.

"Thank you. I've been working on a few more projects, which I hope you get to check out soon."

"I sure will. Well, it was nice running into you. I really should get going. Best wishes on everything."

"Same to you. Good luck with the open house today."

"Thanks." I walked briskly to the self-checkout, which didn't have anyone in line. I paid and rushed out of the store.

"Kaeja," Nate called from behind me before I could make it to my car.

I turned slowly. "Yeah?"

"You dropped your money," he said.

I was in such a rush that I didn't notice that he had stood in the same self-checkout line behind me. He was holding a $20 bill. "Oh, wow. Thank you."

He handed it to me. "No problem. Hey, um, I would love it if maybe we can meet up for a drink or something. You free this evening? We can catch up. I mean, if you're busy, then maybe some other time, but I'm really hoping we can catch up."

"Soraya wanted to have drinks tonight, but I'm sure she won't mind. I'll call her and let you know."

"Okay, keep me posted. If not tonight, you let me know when."

"Okay."

He gave me his card. "Call me."

I nodded with a smile. "Okay, I'll call you."

Walking to my car, I stuffed his card and the money into my purse. I couldn't help but feel a little excited. I placed the tray in the passenger seat and looked up at the sky. It was one of those baby blue skies, not washed-out gray or too cloudy. No signs of spring rain. The dispersed clouds looked like puffs of radiant joy ready to travel in the soft wind. I got into my car with a slight smile on the corner of my mouth.

The open house went so well that we had two offers on the house. The cookies were a hit, and I had Nate to thank for that. I went into the office for a few hours to do some paperwork and to discuss with my client the offers. The offers were both a little lower than she hoped for, but she was going to think about the proposals before coming back with a counteroffer. It was almost 7:00 p.m., and I had spent more hours working than I expected. I texted Soraya.

Me: Hey, girl. I'll be home a little later than expected. Drinks on me tomorrow.

Soraya: No worries. Tomorrow night will be better for me. I'm working on some designs.

Me: Okay. I'll be home in a few.

Next, I sent Nate a text to the mobile number listed on his card.

Me: Hey, it's Kaeja. I'm getting off work. You want to meet at the Royce? They have great happy-hour specials.

Within seconds, he replied: I know exactly where that is. You heading over there now?

Me: Yeah, see you in a bit.

The Royce was a small neighborhood bar where people liked to hang out. They played all the best R&B, and it would be the perfect spot because it wasn't too romantic or too uptight. I made a pit stop into the restroom at the office to pee and freshen up my makeup before heading out.

As soon as I arrived, I looked around and realized I beat him there. I found open seating at the bar, so I ordered a drink. The first taste of an apple martini felt good, and it was much needed. A good cocktail after work always helped me to release some tension.

Nate approached the bar with a smile. "Hey," he said.

"Hey, you," I replied.

"Drinking without me, huh?" he asked, sitting next to me.

"I'm sorry," I laughed. "I should've waited."

"Nah, I'm teasing." He raised his hand to the bartender and asked him, "You got D'Ussé?"

The bartender nodded and replied, "Of course."

"Let me get that, a Red Bull, and lemons, please."

"No problem, boss," the bartender replied.

Nate looked around the bar. "This is a cool li'l spot. I always pass this place and never think to come in."

"Soraya and I haven't been here in a while, but we used to come down a lot. It's a cozy spot."

"Yeah, it is. I like the ambiance." His eyes peered down at me. "Tell me, do you still like to paint?"

I nodded, feeling my cheeks grow hot. I hadn't realized how much he knew about me. "I still dabble here and there. I don't paint as much as I used to. Wow. I'm shocked you remembered."

"How could I forget? We had every art class together since the ninth grade."

"Damn. We sure did. How you even remember that?"

"It's hard to forget the most beautiful girl in school."

I shook my head. "Nah, I wasn't the most beautiful, but thank you."

"Well, to me, you were. What happened to that light-skinned dude you were so crazy about? Um, what's his name?"

"Avian? We broke up like two weeks ago."

"Damn, only two weeks ago? Y'all been together after all these years? Married? Kids?"

I shook my head vigorously. "Never married and zero kids. You?"

"Never married. I've been single for about a year. I was dating here and there, but my work is very demanding. I don't have any kids either."

I didn't know why I had been holding my breath while he gave his answer. As soon as he replied, I exhaled softly. A man with kids wasn't a terrible thing, but I didn't need that kind of situation currently.

The bartender slid over his glass of D'Ussé, a Red Bull, and lemons. "You keeping a tab open, man?"

Nate nodded. "Yeah, and put her drinks on that same tab."

"No problem."

Before he took a drink, he opened his Red Bull and said, "Your breakup is fresh. Is that why you look like you have a billion things on your mind? You seemed a little out of it earlier in the grocery store."

I felt a little embarrassed that I was transparent, but at the same time, I liked a man who paid attention. "Yeah, I took the breakup hard. He cheated on me with . . . you remember Lelee?"

"Big Booty Lelee?"

I hated that everyone knew her as Big Booty Lelee, but that was what everyone called her at Sherman Oaks. "Yeah, and it gets under my skin that he would cheat on me with her of all people."

"I hear you," he said. "All you need is time."

"Yeah," I mumbled, pushing my hair behind my ear. "I don't even like talking about it."

Nate drank and chased it with his Red Bull and a lemon wedge. "Don't worry about it. You don't have to talk about him. You were looking cute as hell earlier in your designer sunglasses. I couldn't walk by without speaking. It wasn't even on some 'look at me now, I'm an actor' type of shit either. It was more like I finally had my chance to step to you. I looked for a wedding ring first. When I didn't see one, I felt like it was my lucky day."

I gave him a broad smile as I ran my hands over my hair, swallowed hard, and replied, "You act like you've been waiting for a long time to step to me."

"I have. Listen, I hope this won't be the last time I see you, Kaeja. I don't want you to get back with Avian, but I understand how that goes. If you end up back with him, I would completely understand. You can't make the mind do what the heart doesn't want."

"I spent thirteen years with him," I replied. "That chapter is over."

"Okay, well, I hope to see you again after tonight."

I blushed and felt so hot instantly. Not hot as in "I want to screw him" hot, but I was hot from blushing. "If my schedule lines up, then we will see if that can be arranged," I said.

I wasn't expecting Nate to want to see me again. Back in high school, we lived in two different worlds. He was the nerdy theater arts kind of guy, and I was the artsy cool kid. I didn't know much about him, but I couldn't wait to find out more. We continued to drink for a couple of hours, and we even shared a few appetizers of fried chicken wings and fries. We made sure that we didn't get too wasted to where we couldn't drive home. He took care of our tab.

"You sure you okay?" he asked, taking a good look at me.

"I'll be fine. Like you said, I need time. You okay?"

"I'm good. That food soaked up the liquor fairly good."

"Yeah, it did. I enjoyed myself."

He opened his arms for a hug, and I hugged him. I fit perfectly into his arms as if I belonged there.

"Thank you for meeting up with me. Drive safe and, please, let me know when you made it home," he said.

"I will. If I don't text you first, you text me when you make it home, okay?"

"I got you," he answered.

As hard as it was to let go of him, we had to let go. With smiles on both of our faces, we got into our cars and went in separate directions toward our homes.

Chapter 24

Kyree

My life without Soraya felt pointless. I was miserable, and I wondered if she was missing me as much as I missed her. I held off on texting or calling, but I was going to have to call her because I still needed to plead my case. I needed to tell her how afraid I was of losing her, and that was why I didn't tell her everything about India. I sent her a text and held my breath for a few seconds before exhaling.

Me: Good morning. I miss you. Please hit me.

I waited for her response, but after I saw that she read it and didn't respond, I couldn't be mad at her. I only had myself to blame. I didn't want to fuck things up like this, and I wanted desperately to work things out with her, but I wasn't going to push her. She wanted space, so space was what I was giving. I didn't care how long it would take, I was going to get my girl back.

I walked out of my house to check the mail. There was a notice from the Department of Child Support Services. Feeling myself frown, I opened the letter as I walked into the house. It was a notice saying that my driver's license was going to be suspended due to nonpayment of child support. I paused.

Wait. What?

How the fuck could she have my driver's license suspended when we didn't have a court-ordered child

support payment arrangement? I knew a couple of niggas who had their licenses suspended over nonpayment
of court-ordered child support, but this was bullshit! I
needed my license because I didn't need any issues with
LAPD if caught driving without it.

My funds were low because I had been spending and
hadn't booked any big gigs since the Chris Brown event. I
was going to have to spend my savings if I wanted to stay
on top of this shit.

I walked out of the house and got into my car. Before I
could back out of the driveway, India called.

"What's up, India?" I asked. "Why the fuck I got a letter
in the mail about nonpayment of child support?"

"Because you haven't given your child a dime since you
put me out."

"You can ask me for anything when it comes to him.
Now you're being petty."

"Fuck you! I shouldn't have to call and ask for shit!
Money should be automatically hitting my account regardless."

"Whatever. I'm on my way to the child support office
right now to pay this shit. They trying to suspend my
license, you know that? Why didn't you call me before
you went to them?"

"Look, I didn't know they were going to do that. How
about you bring three hundred dollars, and I'll call child
support to tell them you don't owe me anything. Cool?"

"Cool. Where are you? You at your mom's?"

"No. I'll text you the address." She ended the call.

I pulled up to the closest Chase and pulled money out
of my savings. Walking back to the car, I hit the address
through India's text and followed the GPS for about
thirty minutes to a rundown motel off the Sunset Strip.

The motel was one of those spots where men with
round beer bellies went to fuck other niggas' wives while

making empty promises. I watched a hooker bring her john into one of the rooms on the raggedy second floor. The entire motel looked like the building inspector was either bribed to pass it or drunk. I scowled and shook my head. This was no place for my son to be if he was here with her. I prayed he was with her mother. I drove by a few cars that belonged in a junkyard.

I parked and got out of the car, looking around at this crazy-looking place. As I texted India for the hotel room number, my eyes went straight to the litter from cheap fast-food meals in the parking space next to me.

India: Room 210.

I walked to the external concrete stairs that led to the second floor. As I walked up and on the second floor, there was a screaming match going on in another room and a hollering baby in another. I passed a few more doors before I got to the room and knocked on the door.

She answered it and let me in. I walked inside and handed her some money. "Here."

She nodded. "Thanks. Is this your money or hers?"

"We ain't even together anymore, so I don't know why you ask me that."

She put the money in her bra and crossed her arms. "Just asking. She didn't go for your shit? How does it feel to be rejected? That shit hurts, doesn't it?"

I looked around the room and couldn't help but notice how messed up the place looked. Clothes were all over the area along with fast-food trash. My son's toys were all over the floor, but he wasn't there. Her heels sure weren't job-interview pumps.

"Ay, uh, you been going out clubbing?" I asked.

"Thanks for the money, but you can leave now."

What I saw next on the floor among piles of clothes made my stomach turn, and I felt anger burn inside of me. It was a used condom sitting right on the fucking floor.

"What is that, India?" I pointed at the condom.

Her reddened face said it all as she threw it in the trash quickly. "I gotta pay to stay here, right?"

"Seriously? Where's my son?"

"Don't act like you give two fucks about your son. You kicked me out and didn't seem to care about what I had to do to take care of us."

"You should be ashamed of yourself. What kind of example are you setting for our son?"

She tried to slap me, but I blocked her hand. That didn't stop her other hand for striking me, whipping my face to the left. I pinned her up against the wall by her throat.

She held my hands as I choked her. When I realized what I was doing, I let her go. She caught her breath with tears in her eyes. Why would she resort to selling her body when all she needed to do was get a job? My son didn't need her as a mother. She charged at me, tried to hit me again, but I snatched her by her hair and pinned her down on the ground.

"Don't you fucking try to hit me anymore, India!"

She punched me in the mouth, and I felt the blood inside my mouth. My reflex had me backhanding her twice. I never thought that much anger could erupt from me, and it scared me. My grandmother didn't raise me to hit women. India pushed me to the edge, and I didn't understand why she wanted to see me that way.

I bolted out of there and down the stairs. This shit with India had gotten out of control. The rage I felt to see how she was living was unexplainable. It wasn't an excuse for my behavior, and I needed to clear my head. I kept driving without a clear destination. I drove in silence, mad at myself for letting her get to me.

A text came through, and I figured it would be India talking shit, but it wasn't. It was Soraya, and my heart skipped a few beats.

Soraya: I miss you too. You got time to swing by?

Me: Hell yeah. When? Lord knew I needed her right now. *Please say right now.*

Soraya: Right now. Come over.

My anger started to subside. It would take me thirty minutes to get to her, but that was going to be the perfect amount of time I needed to get my composure in check.

Chapter 25

Soraya

I hated to admit that I missed Kyree, but it was the truth. Two weeks without him gave me some time to evaluate what I wanted out of a relationship with him if I wanted to still see him. I wanted him to be honest, regardless of how he thought I would react. I didn't consult with Kaeja about whether I should give him another chance. If this was going to work, we were going to have to start over and hit that reset button, something I didn't usually do with men. When I was done, I was usually done.

Before I knew it, he was knocking on my door, and we were face-to-face. Without asking if it was okay, he hugged me.

"Soraya," he breathed against my ear with his voice full of blissful ecstasy.

When we parted, he stared at me with sad eyes. He looked downright pitiful without words. His lips slightly parted as if he was trying to say something but then thought about it and changed his mind. As the silence between us attempted to take over, I started the conversation.

"How are you, Kyree?"

"I'm okay. I'm glad you texted me back. I've been thinking about you."

"I've been thinking about you too, to be honest." I closed the door, and before I could say anything else, he swept me up into his arms and placed the deepest kiss on my lips.

His tongue moved from my lips along my neck, and I nearly popped from the inside out. That velvet tongue had me. Kyree had a hold on me so tight. His hands moved to my pants, and I stopped him.

"No, Kyree. We can't fix this with sex. Sit down. We need to talk."

"Okay," he replied as he took a seat.

I sat in the chair next to the couch and said, "Let's start over."

He swallowed hard. "I want that more than anything. Soraya, you and I belong together."

"You really feel like that?" I asked, looking up at him.

"I do."

"You sure there isn't anything else I need to know?"

"Like what?"

"I don't know. I want you to be straight up this time."

"I told you everything. India and I are over. I have custody issues with her that I need to resolve, but you have nothing to worry about. Soraya, I love you."

My feelings for him were strong, but I wasn't ready to say I loved him yet. I was still wounded. I hoped he'd do his best to do better from that point on. Everyone deserved a chance, and Kyree seemed as if he wanted to work this out.

"I do care for you, Kyree, but let's take things a little slower this time, okay? It's going to take me some time to recover. You two have a child and a history before me, so it's not my place to get into your business. I don't want you to feel like you need to lie to me."

"I won't lie anymore or hide anything. I want you to be my woman, Soraya. From now on, I will be honest about everything."

I replied, "Okay. We will take it one day at a time. Thank you for coming by."

"You kicking me out already?"

"Not like that, but you should leave. I'll call you tomorrow morning."

"Like that?"

"Yeah."

"Okay." He stood up and walked toward the door. "You should come by to my place tomorrow night. Let's have dinner. Will that be cool?"

My first invite to his house and I was surprised, but that let me know he was ready for the fresh start. "That will be cool."

"Okay. Good night, Soraya."

"Night, Kyree."

He left, and I locked the door behind him. I smiled, feeling proud of myself for not letting him stay the night. As bad as I wanted him to stay, if we wanted to start over, I was going to have to do things my way.

Chapter 26

Kyree

The old me would've begged to stay, but I cared for Soraya and respected how she wanted to handle us. I was happy she was giving me another chance. My next step was to get my divorce final. I should've told her that India and I were married when she asked me if there was anything else I needed to say to her, but I couldn't bear to hurt her again. It wasn't like I wanted to be married to India anymore. I wanted my love for Soraya to work, so I was going to make sure she would never find out about my marriage. I was even okay if Soraya couldn't tell me she loved me yet. One day, she would say those three words to me a million times.

As soon as I got home, I sent India a text because I was feeling guilty about what happened at the hotel.

Me: I didn't mean to hit you. Please forgive me. We cannot continue to hurt one another. You're the mother of my child. I'm sorry.

India instantly replied: Fuck you! Leave me alone! You lucky I didn't call the police on you, bitch!

I shook my head. She wouldn't call the police because I could call the cops on her for prostitution. When I first met India, I was with her best friend, but she didn't care. When she got pregnant with my son, I broke it off with her friend and married her so she wouldn't have to be embarrassed about being pregnant by her best friend's man. It solved her problems for a while until I reverted to the person I was before I got with her. Being 100 percent faithful was never in the cards. I kept it all the way real with her, and even though she claimed she was fine with me doing my own thing, I realized she was far from okay.

My mind went back to Soraya. I could look at her every single day of my life. That was how beautiful she was. I needed to be careful with how I handled her because she was precious and delicate, much like a flower. I didn't want to cause any more problems, and I didn't want to hurt her, but I had already disappointed her. I needed her to trust me, but that was something I was going to have to build back up.

As I lay on my bed, my mind drifted off about all the freaky shit she let me do to her like choke her, spank her hard, and the way she deep throated me. There were no limits to what I could do with her, and that was what I had been missing in my relationship with India. India was too reserved and would only consider sucking my dick if she felt comfortable with it, but even then she would back out if it when I really wanted her to do it.

I hated comparing India to Soraya because sexually Soraya's game was off the charts. India was the mother of my child, my prima donna, but when it came to the ideal marriage, Soraya even seemed like she had India beat there as well. Soraya and I clicked, and our chemistry was like a stick of lit dynamite. I loved the way she carried herself, and the way she designed clothing was terrific. She was ambitious with her goals. Not everything that she wanted to obtain in life had shit to do with me, and I loved that. Soraya was independent. I hoped that one day she would be Mrs. Kyree Kirk. That was where my thoughts were, but I was going to have to get rid of the current Mrs. Kyree Kirk first.

Though I knew I hadn't told her everything about India, I promised to be honest from this day forth. If she wanted to know things about India, I would tell her, but only if she asked. Some things were better left unsaid, I felt. To be honest, I knew nothing about her past relationships, and she didn't volunteer them. I felt like Soraya was the one I could do right by. Knowing that I could never be a real man for India was something I couldn't change.

I was going to figure out a way to keep peace with the women in my life. It would be best for me to love Soraya hard and to give India space.

Chapter 27

Kaeja

"When can I see you again?" Nate asked over the phone while I was on my lunch break. "I can't stop thinking about you."

I giggled into the phone, "We had so much fun at the bar the other night. What you have in mind?"

"Come have dinner at my place tonight if you're free."

"I'm free."

"Cool. Will around six be cool?" he asked.

"That's perfect. I can come straight after work."

"Okay. I'll text my address."

"See you soon."

"Later."

I ended the call and ate my salad in the break room. I could not wait for work to be over. I told Soraya about how I ran into Nate at the grocery store. She couldn't believe how famous he was becoming in his acting career. I couldn't believe it either. The rest of my workday seemed to drag, and it was probably because I couldn't wait to have dinner with Nate.

Driving into the gated community, I smiled because I had sold a home inside of this community a year previously. I was awfully familiar with the luxurious homes, and it impressed me that he owned one. My Mercedes came to a roundabout with a fountain at the center, and I swept around it. The white house was topped with an elaborate roof. There had to have been fifty windows on the front of the house alone.

I parked my car and walked up to the stairs to his front door. He answered the door with the dimpled grin before I could ring the doorbell.

"Hey, beautiful," he said.

"Hello, handsome."

We hugged briefly before he closed the door behind me. "I have an apple martini waiting for you. Take your shoes off and make yourself comfortable. Let me give you the tour."

I kicked off my heels and followed him around his four-bedroom, three-bathroom, two-story grand home. The way my toes felt in his plush carpet had me feeling like I was walking on soft clouds. "This is a beautiful house, Nate."

"Thank you. I've been here for about a year now. These are brand new."

"Yeah, I sold a home around the corner from here not too long ago."

"Oh, that's cool. How was work today?"

"Work was work. I need to text Soraya to tell her I'll be home late."

"Is Soraya still dating Jacoury Morrant?"

I laughed, "Damn, you remember everything from Sherman Oaks! No, she and Jacoury broke up years ago. He just got out of prison, what, like two months ago?"

"Really? I thought I remember seeing something in the paper about his charges. Man, he was doing so good at UCLA, I knew I would see him in the NBA."

"Trust me, we all thought so."

Nate led me to his dining room where my apple martini and a prepared Italian dinner of spaghetti, salad, and breadsticks were waiting. We laughed and enjoyed dinner. I helped him wash the dishes, and we went to the couch to talk some more. My eyes felt so heavy as I yawned.

"If you're too tired to drive home, you can sleep in my guest bedroom."

"Oh, Nate, that's so sweet of you. I'll be good to drive home."

"You sure? You worked long and hard today. You've had a few apple martinis."

He was sweet for not wanting me to drink and drive. Nate was so down to earth and humble, never arrogant. I was glad that he wasn't trying hard to push up on me. There was sexual tension, and I wanted to fuck him, but I was usually the type who liked to plan for everything, and things needed to make sense when it came to sex. I felt so free, so brand new.

"I'll stay," I said with a shy grin.

His eyes scanned mine quickly to see if I would change my mind, but my mind was already made up. He said. "I want you to be safe. When you wake up in the morning, come and knock on my bedroom door. If you decide to leave at that point, then I'll see you to your car." He bit his lower lip, and his deep dimples deepened.

I held myself together because I was going to take my time getting to know who Nate had grown up to be. We hit it off, but that didn't mean that I had to move fast and sleep with him.

"Let me show you to the room so you can get some rest."

"Okay," I replied.

"Here you are," he said as he opened the door and turned on the light. "Let me know if it's too cold or hot in here and I'll adjust the temperature. If you need to wash up, there's an adjoining bathroom right through that door. I have a white T-shirt you can get into if you like."

"Thanks. The temperature is fine in here."

"Okay good. I'll be right back."

I smiled as I sat on the soft bed. That mattress felt heavenly. I bet it was a pillow top. I lay back and looked up at his ceiling as my head sank. I let out a deep sigh. This bed felt better than mine at home did. I was funny when it came to sleeping in any bed other than mine. I'd adjusted to Avian's bed once I moved in with him, and then I'd readjusted to my own since being back home. I didn't think I would feel comfortable in Nate's guestroom.

His white feather down comforter was beautiful. I liked the plants he had in the corner. The room was elegant yet simple. It smelled like fresh linen. My eyes closed, and I heard myself snore. I couldn't stop my heavy lids from staying closed. I was asleep before he could bring me that T-shirt.

Chapter 28

Soraya

My designs were selling out fast on my website, making me feel like my clothes were worthy enough to be on display in stores one day. I felt like a superstar. After the successful fashion show and the promotion of my online store, people were ordering things left and right over the next month.

Kyree thought it would be the perfect time to look into getting another vendor so that I could provide some accessories to go with my clothes. He couldn't have been more right. That was precisely what I needed to take my line to the next level.

I was at my kitchen table, going over things for my online store while Kyree observed from over my shoulder.

"I have the perfect distributor in mind," he said.

"Cool. Hit 'em up ASAP."

Keys jingled at the front door before it opened. Kaeja strolled into the house with this soft, heavenly look in her eyes. It was as if invisible hearts were trailing behind her. I looked at the time on my computer. Ever since she started seeing Nate, this was how she entered our spot.

"Hey, y'all," she said as she flopped down on the couch.

"Hey, lady," I said with my eyebrow raised. "Another exciting time with Nate?"

"Yeah," she sighed in a lovestruck tone. "Hey, Kyree."

"Hey, Kaeja."

"You two have sex yet?" I asked.

"Not yet."

"What?" I scowled. "Kaeja, you've been hanging with Nate for a month, and you haven't slept with him yet?"

"Nope," Kaeja replied.

"Damn. Well, it seems like you've been having a wonderful time. You must really like him."

"Nate is a sweetie. We're having dinner tonight at one of his favorite Chinese restaurants." Kaeja bit on her lower lip while trying to suppress her smile, but it wasn't working. Kaeja started grinning so big that it nearly took up her whole face.

"Ooooh, nice. Where y'all going?"

"I don't know yet." Kaeja got up from the couch. "I am going to take a nap before my dinner date." She went into her bedroom and closed the door softly.

"Kaeja looks so happy. That's good," Kyree said.

"Good people deserve true happiness," I replied.

"I agree. Hey, babe, I have an idea. You should have a photo shoot for your clothing line."

"Hmmm. I've wanted to do something like that. It's long overdue. I swear there isn't enough time in one day to do everything that I think of."

"I have a homegirl who's a dope-ass photographer. I'll link you up with her."

"Cool. What's her name? I might know her."

"Her name is Journey."

"No, I don't know her. Does she have a portfolio online that I can look at?" I asked with excitement.

He reached over me to type the photographer's Instagram page, Journey Fulfilled. He clicked on her website from her page, and I fell in love instantly with her photos. I could envision the shoot we could do together. She was extraordinarily talented with her lens.

I leaned my head back to kiss him. He kissed me. Kyree knew exactly what Paradise You needed. He was so attentive when I talked about my passion.

"Thank you for being so supportive," I said. "You have some of the best ideas."

"No problem. It's my pleasure. I'll let you know what she says after I get in touch with her."

"Okay cool. I'm going to start making calls to a new vendor right now. I'm too excited. Thank you, babe."

He winked at me.

Chapter 29

Kyree

Journey's photography skills were exactly what my girlfriend needed to make her fashion line even hotter. As a promoter, I networked with all types of people. I made some mistakes by mixing business with pleasure a few times in the past, and Journey was one of those people. I wouldn't say it was a mistake. I had no regrets about anything that I did, but I wondered how she would feel about me contacting her after a few years of not speaking. I only knew that she was still doing photography through her Instagram.

I'd met Journey six years ago at a club called the Lash. I'd spotted her from across the room. She was rocking her short pixie cut and light brown skin. She was lean and had toned legs as she wore a white spandex dress that was clinging to her body like some Saran Wrap. I didn't mind getting lost in all her beauty because she was that nice to look at. She was unbelievably cute. She took photos for the club and handed out her card, letting everyone know where they could see their picture on her website. That was how she grew her clientele. She took pics for the club to advertise on the club's website, but she also did it to gain customers for herself.

It wasn't one of my events, so I hadn't known who she was. I'd walked away from the conversation I was having with a lame cat who was trying to get me to throw an event for his birthday, and I went over to introduce myself to her.

"Hey there. I don't think we've met. My name is Kyree Kirk."

Once she'd laid eyes on me, she smiled and said, "I know who you are. King-Live Presents is well-known in Hollywood. You throw some of the best parties. You have a good reputation and . . ."

I'd noticed the way her eyes sparkled. I wasn't blind when it came to recognizing when women were feeling me. "And what?"

"I know all about you."

I'd stared at her, surprised. "Okay. I'm shocked you heard of me."

"Don't be. Everyone knows you around here. You're India's dude, right?"

At that time, India and I weren't married yet, but she was pregnant with Kai. "Yeah," I'd answered honestly.

Journey had eyed my casual black Gucci attire for the night, starting from my toes up to my head. I loved Gucci. It was fashionable and comfortable, and women took a second look when I wore it. I'd smiled as I stepped aside to watch her take a few pictures of people partying. I tried not to appear as if I was sweating her hard. Every time she looked back at me, her eyes were flirting with me. I waited patiently for an opportunity to continue our conversation, but I didn't have to wait exceedingly long. She came back my way.

"How you doing tonight?" she'd asked.

"I'm good. What's up with you?"

She'd licked the top of her lip and grazed her top teeth with her tongue, then replied, "Nothin'." She had a set of the dreamiest eyes I had ever seen. They were profound, an intense brown color. Her lips were full and had the reddest shade of lipstick applied.

"What's your name?" I'd asked.

"Journey."

I'd shaken her hand after she extended it. Her camera was hanging around her neck. "Nice to meet you, Journey."

"Same here."

Silence mixed with sexual tension had blanketed the air. I couldn't think of what else to say, and she went right back to taking more photos. She had flashed me a confident smirk before she smiled. She was aware that I couldn't take my eyes off her.

Some clumsy drunk girl had bumped into her, spilling her newly filled drink all over Journey's dress and camera.

"Shit," she'd cursed. "This is an expensive piece of equipment!"

The drunken girl had kept apologizing. "I'm sorry! I'm sorry! I'm so sorry! Oh, my God! My bad, girl!"

Journey had eyed the girl without saying anything else, looking like she wanted to beat her ass. The girl quickly staggered as far away from her as she could.

Being the man that I was, I went over to the bar to grab some napkins. I knew it wouldn't be much to dry her dress, but I'd at least wanted to get her camera dry. As I went to hand her the napkins, my hand grazed hers. We both felt a spark between us. I smiled, but Journey frowned.

"That fuckin' bitch," she'd said as she wiped off her camera. "Ooooh, if that bitch fucked up my camera, I'm gonna find her and do some damage to her face."

"Let me find out you're Laila Ali up in this bitch," I'd laughed.

She shook her head and chuckled to herself. Damn, her laugh was sexy.

"I hope she didn't ruin your dress. I would get it dry-cleaned as soon as possible. Matter of fact, let me take care of that bill for you, and if she fucked up your camera, I'd buy you a new one."

"This camera cost me a thousand dollars. As far as the dress, it's Forever 21, twelve dollars. I picked it up at the last minute," she'd said and sighed deeply. "Well, it was a pleasure meeting you. I must make sure my shit is still working. Nice meeting you, Kyree." She'd started to walk away to head out of the club.

"The pleasure is all mines. Let me know if you need a new camera."

She'd smirked and kept walking.

I'd wondered, *does she think I don't have an extra thousand dollars lying around?* Back then, I did. I had parties lined up for weeks. I watched her leave, silently hoping that I would see her again. Little did I know my prayers would be answered sooner than I thought.

When I ran into her a few days later at Burger King, I didn't take the opportunity for granted. What were the odds that I would see her at Burger King on Sunset Boulevard so soon? Felt like destiny. She was waiting for her order inside, and I had walked in the door. The drive-thru was too long, so I took my chances on ordering inside.

"Well, well, well, Journey," I'd said with a smile as I rubbed my hands together.

She rolled her eyes. "Are you following me, Mr. Kirk?"

"I wish I were, but not at all. How's your camera?"

"It's fine. No damage. Your gesture was sweet, and I'm sure you're relieved to know that you don't gotta come out of pocket now."

"Oh, I wouldn't mind coming out of pocket for you. It would be worth every penny."

A bashful grin had appeared while her cheeks turned red.

"You ready to order, sir?" the woman at the register had interrupted before I could really make Journey blush.

"Hey, don't leave," I said to Journey before I walked up to the counter to place my order.

Journey's order was called, and I noticed that it was to eat inside, so I got mine to join her. We shared tons of laughs, and there was heavy flirting. To my surprise, she didn't ask me about India, and I didn't bring her up, but she told me that she had broken up with her longtime girlfriend. The fact that she had a girlfriend threw me for a loop because she didn't look like a lesbian to me. She clarified that she was bisexual, which was a significant turn-on. I would've loved to get down with two women.

I'd walked her to her car, which led up to her kissing me. Next thing I knew, we were fucking in the back seat of her car. The windows were tinted, so it was inconspicuous. She told me how much she missed having sex with a man and that she hoped it wouldn't be the last time. She promised to keep it between us, and I was down for that.

After seven months of messing around, late nights, and early mornings, India wound up finding out. India did everything in her power to screw things up for me. At first, Journey didn't give two shits about what India thought, but that wore thin fast. Journey couldn't take India's threats and harassments anymore, and my dick wasn't worth it to her.

Things got ugly between us. She wanted me to leave India and I couldn't. We hardly spoke, and she went back to her exclusive girl-on-girl dating.

I was nervous about hitting her up since we hadn't spoken since then. When I called her to see if she would hook up Soraya with a good discount on photos, surprisingly she didn't hesitate to give me a prompt answer. She sounded happy to hear from me. Soraya was making some calls, so I stepped out on the balcony.

"Hey, you. I'm glad you still think of me as the freshest photographer around," Journey said.

"Facts," I said. "You're the hottest photographer in the world."

"You talkin' about my looks or my skills?"

"Take it how you want."

She giggled into the phone. "I'll make sure that your girlfriend's work is beautiful. What happened to India, if you don't mind me asking?"

"We aren't together like that. We raise our son, and that's about it," I said.

"What? That's unbelievable. I heard you two got married after all that drama went down between us," she said.

"Yeah, we did, but things didn't work out. We're getting divorced."

She said, "Well, I'll look at my schedule and let you know what works for me. I'll hit you back to confirm it. Should I call you or her?"

"You can call me. And she doesn't know about you and me hooking up back in the day, so don't mention anything about what happened in the past."

"Trust me. I won't say a word. I get it."

"Thanks. How you been?" I asked.

"I've been happy, drama free."

"Are you're saying you're drama free because you're no longer fuckin' with me?"

"Yeah, and so you know, leaving you alone was my choice."

"Yeah, it was your choice. You kicked me to the curb like I didn't mean shit to you."

"Don't go there, Kyree. I don't fuck with you because of your crazy-ass baby mama. She was doing too much. If I got another death threat, I was going to have to put my hands on that bitch." She wasn't lying. She would've really hurt India.

"Journey, Journey, Journey," I sighed.

"Kyree, Kyree, Kyree. How's Fendi with his fine ass?"

I chuckled. "Fendi stays chasing the bag. I haven't had a chance to catch up with him in a few months. He was in Puerto Rico for a few weeks the last we spoke."

"Nice. Speaking of a bag, I'm still waiting for you to pay me back that six hundred dollars you borrowed, right?"

I rubbed the back of my neck. I had forgotten all about that. "I remember. I'll grab it out of my account and have it for you when you link up with my girl."

"Cool. That works for me. Look, I gotta run. I'll hit you up if my schedule is free, all right?"

"Yeah," I said and ended the call and blew air from my lips. I was going to have to book something soon to pay Journey back the money I owed.

I slid the sliding door open and went into the house. Soraya had her earphones on, listening to music while she worked on her designs. She took them off when she saw me. "Is she available?" she asked.

"She's going to look at her schedule and get back to me."

"Cool."

I kissed her lips. "I'm going to make a few runs. I have to meet up with a club owner to see about this event."

"Okay, baby. See you later."

"See you."

I grabbed my keys and headed out of the apartment. I really hoped this gig would come through, because I needed it.

Chapter 30

Kaeja

After my nap, I woke up refreshed. I looked around my room and realized certain items in my room still reminded me of Avian. I didn't need these things anymore. I got a big trash bag and put the stuffed animals he got me for Valentine's Day into it. The pictures we took at the fair last summer on my dresser mirror went in the bag as well. I didn't want the constant reminder. I took the trash out to the garbage bin, and when I came back into my bedroom, I took a bubble bath. I soaked for thirty minutes or so. I got dressed for my dinner date with Nate.

I arrived at the Chinese food place called Cherry Blossom Garden after another thirty minutes of getting dressed. As soon as I walked into the restaurant, the ambiance sucked me in. It was upscale and fancy with all the elegant Chinese decor.

"Do you have a reservation?" the petite Asian woman asked from behind the podium.

"Um . . ." I paused. I wasn't sure if Nate had made a reservation. I reached for my cell phone in my purse to text him.

Nate approached me from the dining area, so I stopped scrambling. He was looking good in jeans and a blue short-sleeved button-up. That dimpled grin on his face was warm as usual.

"Hey, you," I said.

"Hey," he said. He turned to the lady. "She's with me."

The Asian lady nodded, and he took my hand to guide me to our table. When he pulled out my chair, I caught a whiff of his nice-smelling cologne. It was a different scent from the last time. This one made me want to kiss him, but I would wait later for that.

"I come here a lot," he said as he sat across from me.

"I've never been here before," I answered. From the few glances I had taken from the plates on the other tables, the food looked and smelled fantastic.

"You look good tonight, Kaeja." He smiled.

"Thanks. So do you, as always." I picked up a menu. "What would you recommend?"

"Oh, man, the dim sum and the Peking duck are delicious."

"Hmmm, I'm too scared to try anything that I don't usually get. I'll stick to my shrimp fried rice and egg rolls." I laughed.

He nodded. "I understand. I'll let you taste some of mine." He winked.

Nate was a beautiful person. I didn't know of anyone who was genuinely friendly at his level of celebrity. His friendliness was appreciated, but this wall was still up even though I wanted to knock it down.

As I stared at my menu some more to see if I wanted to have some sweet and sour chicken, a waitress came to our table with a pad and pencil. "Hello. Are you ready to order?"

"You ready to order?" Nate asked me.

"Yeah. I'll, uh, have shrimp fried rice, sweet and sour chicken, and one chicken egg roll. Oh, and can I have green tea?"

"Yes, and you want your regular, Nate?" she asked with a smile.

"Yes."

The waitress nodded and left the table.

"I'm starving," I said.

"Me too. Hey, so I have a movie that I start shooting in England. I want you to visit the set if you can."

I gasped silently. I felt sad that he was leaving and going so far away, but the invitation to visit England sounded so good. Plus I was curious about what happened behind the scenes. I mean, with Avian I went to plenty of industry events, but this was a different level of exclusive.

"When you going and for how long?" I asked, pulling out my phone to look at my calendar.

"I have to leave in a week. I'll be gone for eight months," he said. "That's a long time without seeing you, and I don't want that much time to go by before I get to see you again. Someone may steal your heart, and I'll come home looking like somebody killed my dog."

"You have a dog?" I asked because I didn't remember seeing a dog at his place.

"No, I'm just saying. I would be disappointed because . . . I've had a crush on you since high school. I don't know why I didn't tell you that. That was why I couldn't let you walk out of that store without saying anything to you. I don't want me shooting a movie to miss out on another opportunity to make you mine."

I melted. His words were flattering, and I was feeling him too. "I'll make sure that we don't lose touch. I'm not in any rush to meet anyone."

The waitress came back with my hot green tea and his Coke before leaving again.

"Did you find that you have some vacation time available?" He took the straw out of the paper, put it into his cup, and took a sip.

I picked up the small teacup and held it up to my lips. It was piping hot, so I put the cup down. "Yeah, I have plenty. I haven't taken a vacation in two years. I was saving it for the right time, and I have a passport waiting to add stamps to it."

"I think this is the right time, don't you? I'll cover your expenses. If it makes you feel more comfortable, I'll get you your own room. It would be cool if you can see the work that I do. I will say that being on set takes hours of each day, but there will be times when I won't have to be on set."

"Next week, you said?"

"Yeah. You have a few days to think about it."

"Thank you for the invite. I feel special."

"As you should. I do not bring just anyone with me to work."

I smiled. "I used to go with Avian to work. I hated it at times. Too many women."

"The industry is filled with women, but as men, we have to realize that when we have a good woman, no one can compare. How are you feeling about your breakup these days?"

"When you love someone, it doesn't go away as fast as you want it to. Each day, my feelings for him are slowly leaving."

"Dating someone other than Avian is so new, and your feelings may not be where my feelings are right now, but I'll wait for you. I waited for this long."

Once again, my heart melted. "Nate, why didn't you tell me about your feelings back then?"

"First of all, you would've thought I was crazy. How could little nerd boy tell the most popular girl in school that he had a thing for her? I couldn't compare to the popular football player. You were so madly in love with him. Now is the perfect time to tell you how I feel, though. You're so beautiful, Kaeja."

I giggled and held my heart. He was tugging at my heartstrings. "Thank you for telling me, and thank you for approaching me in the store. Listen, I would love to come to England, especially because I really need a vacation. Let me work my schedule out."

A huge grin spread across his handsome face. "Coo', coo'." He tried to play cool as he rubbed his hands together.

Once our food arrived, I laughed at his jokes, and he smiled at mine. Nate couldn't eat with chopsticks to save his life. Seeing him try was funny as hell to me. He gave up and ate with a fork. I got down with the chopsticks. I tried to teach him, and he got it a little bit, but he preferred the fork.

By the time our waitress came back to the table with the dessert menu, neither of us had noticed that she was even standing there. We were laughing too hard.

"I'm sorry," Nate said to her. "Give us a second to look over the desserts."

She nodded and quickly left.

I busted out into laughter again. "You're hella funny."

He replied, "I'm glad I can make you laugh. You want some dessert?"

Nate looked at the menu as if he didn't know the menu by heart. I picked up the menu. I was too full to eat it, but I wasn't ready for our date to end.

"Banana roll, green tea ice cream. Ooooh, fried ice cream sounds good," I said, reading the menu.

"Fried ice cream is one of my favorites."

"How do they fry the ice cream without it melting?" I wondered aloud.

"They take a scoop of ice cream that is frozen colder than usual, and then they fry it. You'll love it. They sprinkle cinnamon and sugar on top with some whipped cream."

"That sounds good."

The way he looked at me made me feel tingly inside. Something about his gaze had my insides going crazy.

"You want anything else?" he asked as he licked his lips and signaled for the waitress to come back.

"I'm okay with the fried ice cream," I said.

As I watched his lips move while he told the waitress what we wanted for dessert, I couldn't stop my thoughts from wondering what his lips felt like. We had spent so much time together, but we hadn't shared a single kiss.

"After dessert, I don't want to keep you out too late. You have to work in the morning," he said.

"You're fine. I have tomorrow off. What are your plans after you leave here?" I asked.

"I'm going home. Why? You want to come over? That pillow-top mattress is calling your name again, huh? Can you hear it?"

"Ooooh, your guest bed is heaven on earth. If I come to your place tonight, I don't want to sleep there, though."

"No?" he asked with his eyebrow raised.

"No."

He nodded with a grin, noticing the hint. "We can work something out."

We stared into one another's eyes for a moment, and the fried ice cream was placed before us. We ate it, and I couldn't finish all of it. I liked the new yummy experience, but I was stuffed.

I reached for my purse, and Nate said, "I know you don't think I'm going to let you pay for dinner. I won't let you do that. I got you."

"I actually was going for my gum." I laughed. "You got this."

He laughed with a nod. "You're funny."

I laughed again. "Dinner was really nice. Thank you."

"You're welcome." He placed the money on the table and left a tip. "Are you following me back to my place?"

"I sure am."

He grabbed for my hand, and I gave it to him. He rubbed the top of my hand on our way to the front door. Before we could walk out, Avian walked in with Lelee, and I felt as if the room had spun around.

Avian's hair was slicked back into a curly ponytail, and he honestly looked more Puerto Rican than black. He was wearing a nice pair of jeans and a white sweater. He looked too good, so I turned my head quickly away from him. Lelee looked ratchet as usual in that green jumpsuit. Her gold accessories and her lace-front wig were the only things that seemed halfway decent. How could he ever trade me in for her?

My surprise turned into anger, but I didn't show it. The pit of my stomach felt like it had been torched. My night had been so perfect, and I hadn't thought about either one of them. God must've been playing one big trick on me to shove them in my face like this. Instead of crying and feeling devastated, I wrapped my hand around Nate's waist.

Avian looked as if he wanted to say something to me as we made eye contact, but he wound up frowning instead. I was so glad I wasn't alone running into them. I might've reacted differently if I had been. Avian moved his eyes to Nate. After recognizing him, he smirked.

Lelee grabbed Avian's arm overprotectively. "Look, bae, it's Nate from Sherman Oaks," she said with her one eyebrow raised.

"How are you, Lelee?" Nate asked to be polite.

"I'm good. Look how handsome you are now. Wow. He's a good look for you, Kaeja."

"I know," I replied as I flashed a grin, grabbing Nate's hand to walk out of the door. "Y'all enjoy your night."

I couldn't believe how calm I reacted as we walked toward the parking lot. I took a deep breath and exhaled.

"Kaeja," Nate said in a calm voice.

"Yeah?"

"You okay?"

"I'm good."

"Okay. You still coming over?"

"Of course. I'll follow you."

He waited until I got into my car before he walked a few cars over to his. On the way to his house, I felt like turning around, going back into that restaurant, and telling Avian that I was glad his ass was gone. I wanted to scream that I had someone who treated me like a queen, but I didn't need to say it. Avian now knew that I had moved on, and I couldn't help but smile to myself. I was proud, and it felt good. *Fuck them.*

By the time I stepped foot into Nate's home, I wasn't thinking anymore about what had happened. Nate and I cozied up on his couch. He had his arm wrapped around my shoulders, and my head rested against his chest.

Nate said, "Alexa, please play Aretha Franklin's 'Ain't No Way.'"

"Playing Aretha Franklin's 'Ain't No Way,'" Alexa replied.

The music instantly blessed my ears. His music choice was appealing. His soul seemed well over the age of 29. Old-school music wasn't a favorite of mine, but it reminded me of my parents. They played music from the fifties and sixties.

"What you know about that Aretha Franklin?" he asked.

"Oldie but goodie. However, I prefer trap music."

He smiled and nodded. "I like all types of music. I like rap, R&B, and trap music. When I relax, I like to listen to soul. Slow dance with me." He stood up and held out his hand.

"Okay." A slight frown was on my face because I wasn't sure if his old soul would mix with my turn-up swag. However, we slow danced.

I relaxed, rested my head on his shoulder, and I felt like I was in an old-time movie that I used to watch with my grandmother. When I closed my eyes and listened to the lyrics, I felt this sensation. There was something in Aretha's voice that penetrated me.

As I swayed my hips from side to side, he wrapped his arms around my waist tighter. He palmed my face with his right hand. When he kissed me, I let out a long moan. His lips felt so soft like two cotton balls, better than I imagined. As I fed him my tongue, he went for the button on my sequined shorts. As soon as he helped me slip them off, I kissed him harder. Standing in the middle of his living room, he guided me back to his couch.

His body leaned on the top of mine. His kisses engulfed me.

"Wait, wait." I gently pulled away. Although he was the perfect man, I wasn't ready to have sex with him.

"Did I do something wrong?" he asked.

"No, you're perfect. I'm sorry," I apologized. "I . . . I think I should go."

"I thought you wanted to stay."

"I do. It's . . . I'm scared."

"Scared of who? Me? I'm not Avian, and I won't hurt you, but I won't push up on you. At the restaurant, you said you were ready, so I'm quite sure seeing him with her tonight changed your mind."

I sighed and leaned back on his couch. I closed my legs while he sank down to the floor, resting his back against the sofa. He placed his hand on my knee and kept it there.

"It's not you. I like you a lot, Nate."

"But?"

"There is no but. I'm afraid to fall in love again and so quickly. I hardly allowed myself enough time between relationships. I don't want to get hurt like that again."

"This past month with you has been like a dream come true, Kaeja. I would never hurt you, so let me know if the timing is off, and maybe we'll try to connect when you're ready. I care about you, but I don't know if I can handle being pushed away like this. It's like you're punishing me for what he did."

The music playing in the background filled our silence. I reached down to get my shorts. I slipped them back on and buttoned them up. Nate watched me. He stood up and placed both of his hands in his jeans pockets with sadness in his eyes.

"We don't have to have sex tonight, Kaeja. If you want to stay, you can stay."

I knew that if I stayed, we were going to have sex because I wanted to have sex. Nate's kisses created a puddle in my panties, and my pussy was throbbing hard.

"I promise to see you before you go to England," I heard myself say.

"Okay," he replied, sounding disappointed.

"Good night," I said.

"Good night."

I hugged him, grabbed my purse, and walked out of the front door. I sat in my car, thinking I was a fool to turn Nate down. I was over Avian. Seeing him tonight without crying proved that. My heart was pounding as I sat there feeling so dumb. I was scared that Nate would turn out to be a liar and a cheater, but was it fair for me to assume that all men were the same? I didn't start up my car because I really didn't want to go home. I had a good man who was in love with me, had always been in love with me. He didn't deserve this. I got out of my car and walked back up to the door. I rang the doorbell.

After a few seconds, Nate answered. He had a deep frown as he asked, "You left something?"

Without replying, I pushed past my fear, wrapped my arms around his neck, and gave him the most passionate kiss I could stir up. My passion for him released through my tongue. He was a good man, and I deserved a good man. I deserved Nate. He was not Avian. He did not hurt me. I was going to have to love as if I had never been hurt before.

"Kaeja, I can wait for you. I'm not upset."

"Shhhh. Don't talk. Listen to me, I'm ready for you. I'm ready for this. I'm scared, but it's okay. I want to fall in love with you."

"I've loved you from day one. Now that I have you, trust me when I say that I won't blow it."

I threw my lips to his. He closed the door, lifted me in his arms, and carried me to his bedroom, kissing me the whole way.

Chapter 31

Soraya

My cell dinged from a text message alert as I put some final additions on my latest sketch. I grabbed my phone from the coffee table and read the message. It was from Jacoury. I hadn't heard from him since the night I saw him at the House of Blues. My heart was about to beat out of my chest. I'd wanted to call or text him during my break away from Kyree, but now that I was back with Kyree, I didn't need him trying to distract me.

Jacoury: WYD?

Me: Working on designs. Where's your woman?

Jacoury: Told you she isn't my woman. We do not see one another anymore.

Me: What's up?

Jacoury: I need to talk to you. Call me.

I sighed, but I was curious to see what he wanted to talk about. I called him. He picked up on the first ring.

"Hello?" he asked.

"Why you want me to call you?"

Jacoury chuckled. "I don't know why you get at me like this. You called me your buddy at the House of Blues. I can't call and check on my buddy?"

"I mean, I guess you can. Why it take you so long to hit me up?"

"After you blew me off that night, I didn't want to bother you. I came to your fashion show. Bet you ain't even know I was there. I hugged your mom and spoke to Kaeja. You were busy with ol' boy. Listen, I've been hearing things about you and that nigga. You gotta stop seeing him, Raya."

"You crazy," I scoffed. "I'm not going to stop seeing him just because you told me to."

"You don't even know him. Trust me when I say that you don't need to be with him."

"My relationship with Kyree is not perfect, but that's okay. We're working through it. Whatever rumors you heard, I don't even want to hear them. Plus you could be saying anything to get me back."

"Buttercup, as much as I would love to have you back with me, I wouldn't do it like this. Don't tell me you're in love with him."

"Why you say it like that? What if I am?"

"Because you don't know anything about him, Raya. If you really knew this nigga like that, you wouldn't be giving him the time of day. You don't play around when it comes to your heart, so why are you putting your heart on the line like this?"

My guard was up. "You talking about him like you know him."

"I know him better than you do. What you know about him? Tell me. Let's do some fact-checking."

"Well, he has a five-year-old son named Kai. He and his baby mama are no longer together. He's done some things in his past that he was in trouble for, but he did his time. His grandmother passed away and left him some money. He bought a house with it, and he's an event promoter."

"And what else?"

"What you mean what else, Jacoury? That's all I need to know, right?"

"You're missing some key information."

"Key information like what?"

"You know everything about India?"

"Yeah. They were living together. She was pregnant again but lost the baby. He takes care of his son, and that's it."

"Okay, what else?"

"Man, Jacoury, stop playing with me. If you know something, say it. What? They still live together or something?"

"They're married. Did he tell you that?"

I paused and blinked hard. "You got him confused with someone else. Kyree isn't married."

"He's definitely married."

"Kyree isn't married! He would've told me!" I screamed, feeling frustrated. If Jacoury was lying, which to my knowledge he'd never done to me before, I would never talk to him again.

"Well, I hate to be the bearer of unwelcome news . . . Nah, fuck that. He can't have my girl out here looking stupid. Everybody knows that they're married, Soraya. Ask around if you need to. They may have split up, but it's deeper than some baby-mama drama."

"How do you even know all of this?"

"India is Tiff's best friend. I've heard it all. I even heard about you going to the hospital and how you found out about her losing the baby. I didn't think you would still fuck with him after that. Let me ask you this: why is it okay to see him when he's been to jail for way worse shit than me, but you can't give me a chance? We go back, Raya. What makes him better than me?"

Jacoury had a point. I didn't bother to do any research of my own on Kyree when I should've. I took him at his word, and it did nothing but leave me disappointed and heartbroken.

"Hold up," I said as I tapped on my computer to unlock it. I brought up Google Chrome and started my search for marriage records in Los Angeles County.

"What you doing?"

"I'm looking up his marriage certificate if I can find it. Fuck, I don't know his last name."

"Wait, you in love with someone and you don't know his last name?"

"Shut up! You know it?"

"Yup. It's Kirk. Kyree Kirk."

I went to the Los Angeles County records page and entered his name into the marriage certificate field. Lo and behold, his marriage license stared me in the face. I looked up divorce documents in his name and didn't find anything. He was in fact married to India.

"Fuck," I exhaled. "I can't believe this shit."

"You must've found it?"

"Yeah. It's right here."

"Told you," he said. "What you think about him now?"

"I don't know what to say. Thank you, though, for letting me know. Um, you didn't have to, but it must be hard to sit back and watch me make a big mistake like this."

"I'm not judging you, so don't think I am. I want you to do good. You deserve better. I got your back, Raya. I'll always have your back. Even if he weren't married, he's not the kind of nigga you should be with. He's known for using women for money. He and his boy Fendi, shit, them niggas are heartless. They will do and say whatever to knock a bitch."

"He's never gotten a dime from me, and I've never been around Fendi. I met him once, and that was at the House of Blues that night."

"Consider yourself lucky. I'm sure Kyree knows by now that you're too smart to fall for his lies, but then again, I don't put shit past him. I would change all your passwords, make sure your banking information is safe. When you break it off with him, I wouldn't want him to try no shit."

My brain felt like it was overloading. "Look, Jacoury, this is big news. I need some time to gather my thoughts. Can I call you back in a few days?"

"Yeah, I'll be around."

"Okay. Thanks again for the information."

"No problem."

I hung up, and I felt like I had been hit by a raging bull. This shit with Kyree had officially worked my last nerve. I hadn't fully lowered my guard when I agreed to start fresh because something had told me to stay on point to protect my heart. Though this news was disappointing, I was glad to know the truth. I just wished it had come from Kyree instead of Jacoury.

Chapter 32

Kyree

Journey agreed to meet up with me at this little corner bar after the club so I could give her at least half of the money I owed her. I sat on a stool at the bar and ordered a double shot of Patrón. The bartender poured it within seconds.

Downing my drink, I could feel someone watching me. A woman was sitting at one of the tall tables along the wall with a few of her friends. She stared right into my eyes, penetrating me as if she had laser vision, so I looked away quickly.

As I looked toward the front door to see if Journey had arrived yet, the woman decided to make her way over to me. She had bronze-colored skin and smoldering eyes, not to mention her curvaceous body in that cocktail dress, her diamond earrings, and rings screamed that she had a lot of money. She was on the prowl, looking for a young man to get her cougar paws on. The old me wanted to jump out, but the new me wouldn't let the nigga come out.

"Shit," I said under my breath, hoping she would go away.

"Hello, would you like another drink?" she asked.

"Oh, no thanks."

"Bartender, please give this man another drink of whatever he's having, and I'll have another topaz martini," she said, never taking her eyes off mine.

The way she looked at me, I knew she wanted me. I played her off as I shifted my body on the stool to turn toward the bar.

"What's your name?" she asked.

"Gucci," I said. I didn't give out my real name to women I wasn't interested in.

Her eyes pierced me some more as she eased on the stool right next to me. This woman was aggressive as hell. "Gucci? Well, it's a pleasure to meet you. My name is Serenity." She licked her lips as she reached for her drink.

The bartender set my glass down in front of me. "Thanks for the drink," I muttered.

She licked the rim of her drink and said, "I don't want to impose, but are you waiting for somebody?"

"Yeah, my friend is late."

"Your friend? Is this a woman or a man?"

"A woman, but she's my friend as I said. My woman is at home waiting for me, though."

"Well, tonight is my lucky night then," she said with a girlish laugh.

"Your lucky night?" She was making me nervous, and I instantly felt like leaving. This was strange. I never got nervous when women hollered at me.

"Your woman is at home, and that makes me lucky because she's not here. How can I get you to come home with me?" She was ready to leave the bar with me to give me some pussy after buying me one drink. Did I look like a cheap piece of ass? She wanted some attention, but she had the wrong nigga.

"You always ask men you don't know to go home with you after buying him one drink? If I pulled that line on you, wouldn't you feel uncomfortable?"

She shook her head as if she wouldn't care if I gave her that same line.

I looked toward the door, and Journey was walking in. Serenity took one look at Journey, and she looked threatened by how beautiful and young Journey was.

Journey's hair was faded, nearly bald, and it was blond like she was channeling Amber Rose. Her natural make-up and long eyelashes were lovely, and her glossy lips looked pouty. Even without hair, Journey was gorgeous. Not to mention, the short fur she wore with her skinny jeans made her look like a supermodel.

"Wow, is that your friend?" Serenity asked.

"Yeah. Hey, Journey," I said with a big smile. I got up to give her a hug. I was relieved that she could save me from the thirst trap Serenity was trying to set.

"I see you still don't know how to be anywhere without women vying for your attention," Journey interrupted with a sly grin on her face.

"I couldn't help myself," Serenity said. "He's too fine to be sitting at the bar alone."

"Thanks again for the drink, Serenity, but would you mind letting my friend sit right here?" I asked.

"Oh, no, I don't mind. It was nice meeting you both, but before I go, Gucci, would you like to exchange numbers?"

"No, thank you. I told you that I'm taken."

Serenity shrugged and hopped off the stool to return to her friends with her drink in her hand.

Journey laughed as she sat in the stool. "Whoa. You still got it, huh?"

"Man, listen, she weirded me the fuck out. You want a drink?" I asked.

"Shit, yeah. Get me a lemon drop. I can't believe I witnessed you reject a bad one. Not any bad one, a rich, older bad one. One who was ready to show you how strong her cougar game is."

"Whatever." I turned to the bartender. "Excuse me, can I get a lemon drop for the lady?"

"Sure thing," he replied.

"You must really like this Soraya girl," Journey said.

"I'm in love with her. I finally found someone I can settle down with."

"You mean to settle down like settle down, settle down?"

"Hell yeah."

"Whoa, I'm officially speechless. The world must be ending. I never thought that I would see the day when I would hear those words come out of your mouth."

"You still got jokes, I see."

The bartender slid her drink to her.

"Well, the idea that you can be committed alone is quite interesting, because the old Gucci would've never turned down a free drink and some rich pussy."

"I didn't turn down the drink, but I sure did turn down that pussy." I laughed. "Look, I don't live like that anymore. That's Fendi's shit."

"I see. What's really up?"

"Oh, here." I dug into my pocket to give her the $300. "Look, that's only half of it, but I wanted to at least start paying you back."

She took the money from me. "Thanks. I appreciate it. When does your girl want to do this photo shoot?"

"As soon as possible."

"Okay cool. What does India think about you and Soraya?" Journey asked.

"Come on, Journey. Don't do that."

"What? I'm curious. Anyway, even if I asked you to leave here with me, would you?"

I licked my lips at her offer. It was one hell of an offer, and I knew how wet and tasty her pussy was, but no one could compare to Soraya. No one. "Nah, I wouldn't," I replied.

She raised her glass to me. "Here's to growing up."

We clinked glasses. "To growing up," I replied.

"I'm proud of you," Journey said with a smile.

"Thank you. That means a lot to me."

"I'm saying I like the new Kyree. Look at you, still wearing Gucci everything though. Nothin' like a grown-ass man in Gucci, huh?"

I chuckled. I liked the sound of that. I was a grown-ass man.

After leaving the bar, I headed straight to Soraya's. I texted her to let her know I was on my way, and she said the door would be unlocked. When I walked into her bedroom, she was sitting straight up in the bed, looking at me as if she were mad at me about something.

"What's up, babe?" I asked as I put my coat in her closet. "You can't sleep or something?"

I tried to give her a kiss, but she pulled away. "Kyree, you smell like liquor."

"What?" I asked with a frown.

"You drunk?"

"I'm not drunk. What's the matter with you?"

"Are you married?" she came right out and asked me.

It would only be a matter of time before she found out the truth, but I was hoping that I'd be the one to tell her. My mind was racing. *Wait, who told her?* I wondered if India contacted her.

"Who you hear that from?" I badgered.

"Is it true?" She searched my eyes, looking for a sign that would prove the crazy notion to be true. "Are you married to India?"

"Depends on who you heard it from," I replied, feeling upset.

"Your answer depends on who the source is? What kind of shit is that?"

"First of all, who told you that?"

"It doesn't matter," she exploded as she tossed the covers off her.

I looked at her with a perplexed look on my face. "It does matter!"

"It doesn't matter if everyone in Los Angeles knows that you're married to India except for me? You know that marriage licenses are public record, right?"

I swallowed the lump that felt like a mass in my throat. I'd forgotten about that. Most of the women I dealt with already knew that I was married. This was the first time that I had gone this long without telling the truth on my own.

Soraya snatched a piece of paper from the dresser and waved it in my face. "Your lying ass is married to India. The proof is right here! This is your license in case you want to lie about it, you piece of shit!"

I snatched it from her and stared at it as if I had never seen it before. "Okay, look, hold on one damn minute. Can you sit down so I can tell you my side of the story?"

"Your side of the story? Your side of the story doesn't matter when your side of the story is bullshit! I'm done. It's over, Kyree! I can't even cry anymore because I'm tired."

I replied calmly, "It's not over, baby. Don't say that."

"It's very much over, Kyree! Go home to your wife and your son!" Soraya went to the closet and pulled out a suitcase. "Your shit is already packed up."

She wasn't lying. The few things I had in her closet were packed up in one of her suitcases. Shit, she was serious.

Before I put my coat back on, I said, "I want you to know that India doesn't mean shit to me anymore. Our marriage was over a long time ago. So what if it wasn't over on paper? Doesn't seem like you really love me because you're willing to walk away so easily. It's cool, though. I'll leave. To think tonight I passed up on some pussy because I love you."

"Nigga, I don't give a fuck what bitch was trying to hop on your young dick! Never again will I fuck with someone so immature. Get out!"

I grabbed the suitcase and left, feeling pissed the fuck off. Whoever had told Soraya had better hope I didn't find out who he or she was. I didn't do well with anyone trying to fuck up my happy home.

Chapter 33

Kaeja

I came home after I made love to Nate. His bed was one of the plushest comfortable beds I had ever lain in, but I didn't want to spend the night yet. I needed air to really think about what I wanted to do. Nate was sent from heaven, but I was good with taking our time. Nate was nothing short of amazing. He was just what I needed to take my mind off Avian.

When I walked into the apartment, Soraya was shouting, cussing Kyree out.

"Go home to your wife and your son!"

I stood in the hallway. He was married? I felt like bursting into the room and cursing his ass out myself. To think that Soraya tried to have a fresh start with him and he still didn't come clean. What a fucking piece of shit!

Her bedroom door opened, and Kyree stormed past me to the front door. He acted like he didn't even see me. I walked into the entryway of her bedroom. She was staring off into space with her arms folded across her chest.

"You okay?" I asked.

She faced me. "Yeah, girl. This shit is for the birds. I guess you were right about internet dating. It sucks. But you know what? I feel like all of this taught me that I was too hard on Jacoury. Accepting Kyree's flaws has helped me see that Jacoury's time in prison was the only thing I didn't like. He never cheated on me. He never lied to me. He made a mistake with the law, and I abandoned him. I'm a horrible person."

"Raya, you had every right to feel the way you did about Jacoury doing time. You couldn't do it. He's home now, though, and he's still crazy about you. To be honest, you wouldn't allow yourself to love Kyree anyway because your heart is still with Jacoury."

"Well, Coury was the one who called and told me everything."

"Damn. Avian didn't mention anything about Kyree being married, but I'm not sure if he was aware of it. You sure you good?"

"Fuck him. I thought being with Kyree would change the way I feel, but it hasn't. I tried hard to make myself love Kyree. After Jacoury called and told me about Kyree, I kept replaying the night at the House of Blues in my head, and how different it would've played out if I had been all over Jacoury. I sat here for two hours thinking about how good he looked and how my knees buckled when I saw him. A part of me is relieved that I don't have to try to force myself to love Kyree, because I will always love Jacoury. Am I crazy?"

"No, you're not crazy. You convinced yourself that you could never love anyone who ever did time, but Jacoury is a good man, Raya. It's not too late to get that old thing back. Get some rest. If you need me, I'm here," I said.

"Thank you, boo."

I walked out of her room and closed the door behind me. It was time for both of us to stop wasting our time with men who didn't deserve us. Jacoury had learned from his mistake with the law, and he loved Soraya with everything he had. Jacoury was nothing like Kyree.

As I entered my bedroom, I sent Nate a text message.

Me: I'm home.

Nate: I'm happy you made it safely. Good night, beautiful.

Me: Good night.

I set my phone on my bed and stripped out of my clothes. I didn't want to overthink what was happening between Nate and me. I was going to go with the flow and let each day build a painting until I felt confident that when I was with him, I was a better and happier version of myself. I could only ever get to know him over time.

My ringing phone woke me up. Nate's name was flashing on the screen, and that brought a smile to my face. "Hello," I answered.

"Good morning. Did I wake you up?" Nate asked.

"Yeah, but it's okay. Good morning, handsome dimple face."

"Good morning, my queen. I got some news, and I wanted to share it with you. It's kind of good and kind of bad at the same time."

"What's up?"

"I have to be in England earlier than expected. I have to leave tomorrow, so I wanted to see you before I go."

Sadness greeted me. I didn't want him to go so soon. "Oh, wow. Well, it's a good thing to start working on such an exciting project."

"But it's not good because I want to spend more time with you. The good thing is that I'll be gone for five months instead of eight."

"That's good. What do you want to do today?"

"How about a movie or something?"

"Sounds good to me. You can pick me up. What time should I be ready?" I asked.

"Let's catch a matinee around eleven, and I'll be there about an hour before the show. That'll give me time to pick you up and us to get there."

"All right. I'll be ready."

We ended the call, and I jumped out of bed, made it up, brushed my teeth, and washed my face before I went into the kitchen. The house was quiet. I figured Soraya was still sleeping, but she was on the couch, sketching.

"Good morning," I said.

"Good morning." She was concentrating on her sketch, but then she looked up to smile at me. "How'd you sleep?"

"Pretty good. You?"

"It was a rough night, but I got through."

"I hear ya. You want some coffee?"

"Nah, I got some iced pomegranate tea over here with a shot of vodka."

"Vodka in the morning, I dig it," I chuckled.

Soraya gave a half laugh as she sipped her concoction.

Soraya's phone rang. It must've been Kyree, because she sent him straight to voicemail. The coffee took a few minutes to brew, so I grabbed a banana and a blueberry muffin from our snack area. When the coffee was ready, I poured myself some and added caramel and vanilla creamer.

"You heading to work?" she asked.

"No. Nate has to go to England for a movie, and he leaves tomorrow, so I'll probably be spending the day with him."

"Damn. That sucks."

I peeled my banana. "Yeah, it kind of does, but he invited me to visit him out there."

"Will you be going to visit him in England?"

"I plan to go. I don't know when yet. I have more than enough vacation time to use."

"Kaeja, how can you not get all hyped up? Girl, I'm lightweight jealous. You got you a li'l celeb over there and shit."

I shook my head. "The crazy thing is that he's so normal and down to earth. It's unbelievable."

"Do you remember the time he asked you to the homecoming dance freshman year?"

I frowned because I didn't remember. "No, he didn't ask me."

"Yes, he did. I remember. We were in the library, and he looked like he had worked up the courage to ask you. You acted like you didn't hear him. Poor guy ran out of the library so quick." Soraya shook her head. "I figured you were ignoring him."

"That's because I didn't hear him. I don't even remember," I replied, feeling a little bad. "Oh, man, how can he still like me after that?"

"How can he not? You were the most popular girl in school."

"And so were you," I reminded her.

"Only by default 'cause I'm your best friend."

"Whatever," I laughed.

"Jacoury called me this morning, and we talked."

As I poured a cup of coffee, I replied, "Mmm-hmmm. What he say?"

"He said he's not over me and he's still in love with me."

"Did you tell him that you're in love with him still and you never got over him either?"

"No. I wanted to, but I feel like I don't want to give in so easily."

"I know exactly what you mean." I ate my muffin and finished my banana. "Welp, I'm 'bout to get dressed and head on out for my movie date."

"Okay."

"He's coming to pick me up, and I want him to come in and say hi."

"Oh, shit, well, let me get out of this headscarf and put on my bra. I'm glad you told me," she said.

I laughed and sashayed to my bedroom with an upbeat tempo with my coffee cup. I quickly showered, dried off, and rubbed in shea-butter cream all over my body. I slipped into a red and black maxi dress before applying curl pudding to my curly weave to give it shine and to make the curls snap back into place. While I was putting on the final additions to my makeup, I heard the doorbell ring. Perfect timing, because I was ready. On my way out of my bedroom, I picked up my purse. I sprayed on a little Bath & Body Works Beautiful Day.

Soraya let Nate in. She hugged him. "Hey, Nate. Look at you."

"Hey, Soraya. How you been?"

"Damn, your dimples are still hella deep. It's good to see you."

"Same here." Nate smiled at Soraya before his eyes landed on me.

"You work out?" Soraya asked while taking a good look at him.

"Don't harass my date," I said.

"Am I harassing you?" Soraya asked him.

"No," he replied with a cute little chuckle.

"Harassing him would be me asking him for an autograph. Wait, can I get an autograph really quick?"

"Sure."

She skipped into the kitchen for a piece of paper and snatched a pen out of a drawer. He followed her into the kitchen and signed it for her. I laughed at how silly Soraya was acting. I hadn't thought to ask Nate for an autograph. Not because I didn't think he was star quality. I just hadn't thought of it.

"Thank you." Soraya beamed. "Nate grew up, Kae, and he's lightweight famous. Imagine that!"

He chuckled again. "You're funny. I'm still Nate. You ready, Kae?"

"Yeah. Let's go," I said. "Bye, Raya."

"Bye. Y'all have fun," Soraya replied.

We headed out the door. As we walked down the stairs to his car, he said, "Soraya hasn't changed a bit. She still looks the same."

"True. She does."

He opened the door for me, and I got in while Nate walked around to the driver's side. I started thinking about how much I would miss seeing him while he was gone. I was curious to see how much we would keep in contact while he was away.

We rode to the Regal L.A. Live Cinema on West Olympic Boulevard. The thought of his hands roaming all over my body rushed over me. After he parked in the parking garage, we got out. Before we could walk to the theater, I wrapped my arms around him.

"Mmmm, you smell good," he whispered as he caressed my back with the tips of his fingertips. As he pulled me closer into his chest, my breasts pressed up against him. My heart fluttered at the sound of his voice and the feeling of his breath so close to my ear.

I whispered in his ear, "Thank you. We should skip the movie and go to your place."

Nate grinned from ear to ear. He bit his lower lip before he replied, "Yeah?"

I placed my hand on the side of his face and leaned in for a kiss. As soon as his lips met mine, I didn't want them to leave me. My lips found his chin and his neck. I licked his neck, and he quivered.

"Shit. Fuck this movie. Let's go."

We got back in the car, giggling and laughing like teenagers.

Chapter 34

Kyree

Soraya wasn't answering any of my calls, so I pulled up Facebook on my phone. I put her name in the search bar, and her name didn't come up. I searched through my friends list, and she was no longer my friend on Facebook. *Did she block me?*

"Fuck," I mumbled as I dialed her number. That time, I went straight to her voicemail. "Soraya, this is Kyree. Call me, baby, when you get a chance, okay?"

I ended the call, feeling like a straight sucka for trying so hard. I'd never had to work this hard to fight for a woman. I usually kept it pushing and moved on to the next, but this time, I felt this tugging at my heart. I paced my house, looking at the divorce papers I signed. The last step was to find India and have her sign them so we could get this shit over with.

While in thinking mode, I grabbed my keys and took a drive to In-N-Out Burger. I was starving. The place was packed any day of the week. As soon as I pulled up to the drive-thru, the line was long as fuck. I had no patience when it came to waiting, but the burgers and milkshakes made it worth it. As I waited, I turned my attention to my phone. I scrolled through my newsfeed on Facebook to glance at the posts I had missed. Suddenly, a message came through from India. I was hoping she would tell me she would let me see my son and meet up somewhere.

India: I hate you!

Me: Your feelings are valid, India. I miss my son, and I need to see him.

India: You can see your son at any time. We're at my mom's.

Me: Is it okay if I come by after I grab some food? I got the divorce papers, so I need you to sign them.

India: Why? So you can marry your girlfriend?

Me: No, so we don't have to try to pretend like we want to be married anymore.

She didn't respond for a moment, and the line moved up one car.

India: Come by in the morning. I'll sign them. Kai will be happy to see you.

Me: Okay. I'll call before I come.

India: A'ight. TTYL.

It seemed like it took forever for the line to move forward. After ten minutes, I was able to order my food. I was feeling a little better to know that India was in agreement even after what I had done to her. If she had said she never wanted to see me again, I would've had to deal with seeing my son another way. My thoughts went right back to Soraya. I couldn't wait to show her that I was getting divorced. Then there wouldn't be any more issues between us. Being away from her was killing me minute by minute. I would work as hard as I needed, because she was the one I wanted.

Chapter 35

Soraya

I wanted to see Jacoury. I had been thinking about him nonstop, and I needed to tell him face-to-face everything I had felt while he was locked up. I texted him after I showered and got dressed. I couldn't beat myself up for choosing to date Kyree instead of working things out with my ex.

Me: Hey, text me your address. I'm on my way if you don't mind.

Jacoury: Of course I don't mind. Come through. 1121 West Eighteenth.

Me: You hungry?

Jacoury: I will be by the time you get here. You want to go have lunch?

Me: I feel like cooking us a li'l something-something, is that cool?

Jacoury: I don't have any groceries, but we can go to the store.

Me: I'll pick up what I need on my way.

Jacoury: Okay. You coming now?

Me: Yeah.

Jacoury: Okay.

I grabbed my keys and my purse and locked up the apartment. I stopped by Whole Foods on South Grand. I retrieved a cart and went to the poultry section at the back of the store and got a package of chicken breasts. From the

deli, I got sliced Swiss and American cheese. From pro-
duce, I got romaine lettuce, a red onion, a tomato, and a
couple of sweet potatoes to make fries. To complete my
store trip, I picked up mayonnaise, ketchup, Dijon mus-
tard, soft rolls, vodka, pink lemonade, and Sprite for my
cocktail.

I paid for my things, got into my car, and drove to
Jacoury's. He lived five minutes from Whole Foods. I
pulled up behind his black 1995 Jeep Wrangler in his
driveway. I couldn't believe he still had that car. Though
it was a 14-year-old car when we graduated from high
school, he always wanted an R. Kelly Jeep from his
music video for "You Remind Me of Something." Parked
in front of that Jeep was a brand-new black 2019 Jeep
Wrangler Unlimited Rubicon. He'd upgraded.

I got out of my car and adjusted my clothes. His tall,
basketball-playing frame was standing in the open door-
way as I walked up.

"Dang, you were looking out the window for me?" I
teased with a slight laugh.

"No," he said, trying to play it off, but when he looked
into my eyes, he broke out into a huge grin. "Come in."

I stepped inside, and my eyes scanned his place. I
wasn't expecting his home to look so lovely. The last
place I visited was his off-campus apartment, and it was
such a guy's place, hardly any furniture, no pictures on
the wall. This spot had beautiful black art on the walls,
tall vases in the corners, and a gorgeous tan rug in his
living room that accented his mahogany couch.

"This is nice," I said as I moved around the living room.
"You decorate this all by yourself? Or did Tiff help you?"

"Wow. You start in on me early. Nah, Tiff didn't do
none of this. This is all me."

"I see."

"I was going for the modern look," he continued. "I added a li'l art here and there, learned that from my nigga Jay-Z. You lookin' good. Can I get a hug or something? You walk in acting like you nervous or something."

I hugged him briefly and stepped back. He stood there staring at me without responding, but that cheesy grin was still there.

I walked away from him, saying, "Is your kitchen this way?"

"Yeah. Let me take that bag from you."

I handed it to him. His kitchen was clean with a brand-new stove, refrigerator, and dishwasher. He placed the bag on the granite countertop and rubbed his hands together.

"I'm over here about to start dancing like a little kid about to eat. I'm talking about feet-wiggling kind of happy dance," he said as he went into a James Brown kind of movement with his feet.

"Silly. I'm sure my mom and your mom hooked you up, but you haven't had my cooking in a long time. Plus I'm sure that fish-looking bitch you had couldn't cook to save her life."

"So fuckin' mean still. Tiff can cook, and good too, but that's over with. I'm over at my mom's or yours every day after work. You see my six-pack is nearly gone?"

He lifted his shirt and flashed me his stomach. He was lying through his teeth. That washboard stomach hadn't gone anywhere. Heat rushed through my face. I was sure he could see what he had done to me.

I started removing groceries from the bag. "Well, I'm happy our mothers still look out for you. You don't look like you're struggling these days. Nice crib, brand new Jeep. What you do to get all this so fast?"

"While I was locked up, I got my electrician certification. I made some connections before I got out. I was hooked up with a good-ass job. I'm a journeyman electrician, making thirty-five dollars an hour. I repair and install electrical components for residential and commercial job sites. I work with some of the biggest construction companies."

He had a nine-to-five, and that made me feel bad for assuming that he was on some thuggin' shit. He was doing better than I thought he would be. I didn't know what to expect after he did prison time. My fear that he would always be attracted to thug life got in the way. He'd needed me to believe in him, and I'd failed him.

"I'm proud of you, Coury. That's really great."

I pulled his blender from the corner of the kitchen counter and plugged it in. I looked inside to make sure it was clean. I wound up rinsing it out anyway because I didn't know when he'd used it last, even though his kitchen was spotless. Jacoury came up behind me, put his arms around me, and spun me around.

"Buttercup," he said. "I missed you like crazy. Hurt like hell to not see you, touch you, smell you—"

"Coury," I said, feeling frazzled.

He started to unbutton my jeans. "Wassup, Buttercup?"

He inched toward me and placed a kiss steeped in passion on my lips. He hungrily sucked my tongue, and it ignited me. His kiss was the promise of realness and primal desire that lived in both of us. We were reconnected, and there was no need for me to fight what I felt any longer. His lips made their way all over my neck as his thick lips sucked my skin.

I went to his house without the intention of having sex with him. I wanted to be in his company, but I didn't want it to happen like this.

"Wait, Coury. Baby . . ."

He was breathing hard, chest heaving up and down, as he stopped himself from taking off my clothes.

With his arms wrapped around me, I let my heard rest upon his chest as I whispered, "I love you. I never stopped loving you."

His body relaxed as if he had been longing to hear me say that forever. My heart took over my head.

He squeezed me as if he couldn't believe that I was there with him, as if he were too afraid that this moment was all a dream. No one ever felt the way he did in my arms. I already knew Jacoury and I were meant to be together. It was forever or bust, and I was ready for it. We hugged for what seemed like hours though it was only minutes.

Chapter 36

Kyree

I waited outside of India's mama's house in my car for India to come out. Usually, I would've been able to knock on the door, but after what I did, it wasn't cool like that. India told me to meet her there, and I thought she would've been there, but her car wasn't in the driveway. What kind of game was she playing with me now?

When I thought about driving off, India pulled up and got out of the car. I thought Kai would've hopped out of the back seat and run to me, but he wasn't with her. When we made eye contact, I could see the faded black eye that was healing. Pain struck me. I didn't expect to see her face looking that way. I caused that. I swallowed hard as I got out of my car, and she started walking toward her mother's front door as if she hadn't told me to meet her here.

"What's up? Can I see Kai?"

"He went running around with my mom real quick. He'll be here in a minute. Come in." She put the key into the front door. I hesitated, but she left the front door opened for me. Clutching the divorce papers in my hand, I walked up the walkway and entered Sheila's house.

India purposely cut in front of me before I could sit on the couch. She had her intentions for me and knew what she was doing. She wrapped her arms around my neck. She was trying desperately to reconcile this way, but I wanted to prove to myself that I could be the man for Soraya.

I backed away from her, removing her hands. "I don't want you to get any mixed signals. I came here to see Kai and so you can sign these papers."

I handed them to her, but she refused to take them as she crossed her arms around her chest. "You mean to tell me that after she dumped you, you still don't want to be with me?"

"She didn't dump me," I shot back defensively. "I fucked up, but I'm going to make shit right with her."

She rolled her eyes. "Wow. You know what? I'll hit you up when Kai is here. I can't stand to look at your ass right now."

Shaking my head, I walked toward the door. "I'm supposed to have someone serve you with these anyway. Call me when he gets here."

As soon as I stepped on the porch, she slammed the door in my face. I hated that she had to make this shit so damn tricky. I stormed toward my car, got in, and went home. I wasn't going to fight with India. I didn't know what she was thinking, but I couldn't wait for this to be over.

Chapter 37

Kaeja

I made plans to see Nate before his flight to England, but I stayed at the office a little longer than I wanted to close a deal. If I didn't hurry, I wouldn't be able to spend time with him. I sped toward his house so that I could be with him. I wanted to be able to get in as much time as I could with him. I didn't even know how fast I was going because all I could think about was how he made me feel whenever I was with him.

Red and blue lights flashed in the rearview mirror as I was flying through the intersection. The fact that I was being pulled over made me suddenly get nervous. I hated the police.

I looked in my rearview and saw LAPD with flashing lights pulling up behind me. I sat there for at least two minutes before the officer walked up to my side of the car. I sighed and checked my attitude because I didn't need any other problems. I was relieved to see that the officer was a black man as I hit the button to roll down the window.

"Good afternoon, ma'am. You were speeding." The officer seemed friendly, and he was cute with his bald-headed self.

I peeked at him through my black Prada shades. Thank goodness my boobs were giving much cleavage. I didn't mind using my femininity for a worthy cause such as getting out of a ticket. I saw two ways to get through this situation. I could be quiet and take the ticket to go on my way, or I could flirt with him until he decided not to give me a ticket. His eyes seemed to sparkle once I removed my shades.

I stared him right in the eyes. "I'm sorry, Officer. I was so wrapped up in my thoughts that I hadn't noticed how fast I was going." I flashed him a grin before biting my lower lip.

He returned a crooked smile as he stepped closer to the car. He looked around as if he was looking for someone else in the car before his eyes landed back on me. "Ma'am, is this your vehicle?"

"Yes, it is."

"Are you the registered owner?"

"Well, no, it's in my ex-boyfriend's name."

He looked at the car again. "I need to see your license, registration, and insurance, please."

I took off my seat belt and reached toward the glove compartment for the registration. I took my license out of my purse. "My ex-boyfriend bought this for me as a gift a few years ago. We recently broke up, and I haven't gotten it changed out of his name yet," I explained.

Once I handed my license, registration, and insurance over to him, he stepped away from the car and started talking into his radio. What he was saying was muffled, but I managed to zero in on him saying, "I found a reported stolen car. Registration belongs to an Avian Perez. The driver is Kaeja James. She's listed on the insurance."

Stolen? What? "Sir, I didn't steal this car. It's my car."

"Ma'am, I need you to step out of the car and leave your hands where I can see them," he said.

What's going on? I slowly got out with my hands slightly raised. "Um, is there a problem, Officer"—I looked at his nametag—"Bolds?"

He nodded slowly as he took a good look at me. "Seems like the car has been reported stolen. Are you the owner?"

"Are you fucking serious?" I removed my shades and scowled.

He nodded. "Yup."

Avian wanted to act like a bitch because he saw me out with Nate? What a motherfuckin' hater! He had the nerve when he was fucking around with Lelee behind my back. While I thought that this would be a smooth breakup, he was trying to fuck me with no Vaseline.

I looked at the white Mercedes-Benz CLA 250. I loved this car, but was I about to go to jail for something I didn't do?

"He gave me the car for my birthday two years ago. I didn't steal it, Officer Bolds. We broke up, and he didn't ask for the car back. Am I going to jail?"

"No, I'm not taking you to jail. I believe you," he said. "We see this type of stuff all the time. Look, I gotta tow the car. You know someone you can call to pick you up?"

I thought of having Soraya pick me up, but I remembered that she was over at Jacoury's hanging out. I didn't want to bother her, and I for damn sure wasn't going to call my parents. They were probably out of the country anyway. Ever since I'd broken up with Avian, I had been dodging my mother's calls. What would I look like calling her now? I should've gotten the car in my name. I thought about Nate. He was the only person I could call since I was on my way to his house anyway.

"Yeah, I can call someone."

"All right, get your belongings out of the car before the tow truck comes."

"Okay. Am I getting a speeding ticket, too?" I batted my eyelashes at him, praying he would show me some mercy. I really felt like crying, but I kept my composure.

"No, I won't give you a ticket. I'm going to make it easy on you since your ex is being a dick." He turned away from me to talk into the radio to call for a tow truck.

I went to the car and grabbed my purse. I had a few pairs of shoes in the trunk along with an empty duffle bag. As I started to gather my things, I called Nate.

He answered, "Hey. You outside?"

"No. The cops pulled me over for speeding. Avian reported the car stolen with his salty ass. They gotta tow the car. Can you pick me up, please?"

"He did what?"

"He's trying to say I stole the car, but it was a gift."

"Say no more. I'll be right there. Give me the cross streets."

I walked toward the corner to read the cross streets. "I'm at South Fairfax and South La Cienega."

"Okay. I'll be there in six to seven minutes. Are you all right?"

I walked back to my trunk. "Yeah, I'm okay. I'll see you when you get here."

I heard the officer's boots against the pavement coming toward my direction. I grabbed the last of my things, closed the trunk, ended the call, and turned toward the officer.

"Your ride coming? If not, I can give you a ride to your destination," he offered.

"My ride is on the way. Shouldn't be more than ten minutes."

"All right. The tow truck is on the way."

I was highly upset that my car was being taken, but everything was going to be okay. Avian could take that car and shove it up his fucking ass.

The officer handed me back my driver's license as I stood on the curb. I put it back into my wallet and paid attention to the way he was staring at me. His eyes were dancing all over my cleavage. I cleared my throat and put on my shades to get away from his stare. He went back to his car after looking as if he wanted to say something to me. I wasn't sure what he wanted to say. I was ready to get the hell off this curb.

When I saw Nate pull up, I rushed over to his car, and he popped his trunk. I put my things into the trunk. As I walked to the passenger seat, Nate took a good look at the police officer in his side mirror. Before pulling off, he looked at me.

"Are you all right?"

"I'm pissed, but other than that I'm fine."

"That was a bitch-ass move," he said as he pulled away from the curb. "Avian couldn't call you first to at least give you a warning or something?"

"I never thought Avian would stoop this low. I want to call him and cuss his ass out, but it's not even worth it. He can give Lelee my car for all I care. She should feel happy to push the last bitch's ride."

"You have another car?"

"No, but it's not like I can't go get one. I'll worry about that later. Do you think there will be room for me on that flight of yours in the morning?"

He looked over at me briefly before putting his eyes back on the road. "I'll find out for you. You sure you want to go with me and not wait?"

"I'm dead-ass ready to get out of L.A. After what happened, I don't want to be here."

"How long you want to stay?"

"I don't know. I'll wing it. Would you mind?"

"Nah, I don't mind at all." A dimpled smile graced his handsome face.

As soon as we got to Nate's house, he immediately got on the phone to get me a flight. From the sounds of it, he was able to grab me a first-class seat, but it would have to be on the next flight. For me, he moved his own flight so that we could fly together.

"Good news. We're leaving in the morning. I can take you to your house to get your things, and we can come back here. I'm going to call my manager and let her know that I moved my flight. I'll be right back. Make yourself comfortable."

"Okay."

He disappeared into his bedroom, and I picked up my phone to call Soraya. I was hoping that she would answer as I kicked off my shoes.

"Hello," she answered.

"I'm shocked your ass answered. I figured by now that you and Jacoury would be too busy to pick up."

"Please. Jacoury is playing video games. I'm sitting on his couch, using his computer to work on some designs. Feels like old times."

"I bet that's nice."

"What's up with you, chick?" she asked.

"Well, I got off work and was pulled over by the fucking police. I was speeding, but come to find out Avian's ass reported my car stolen. It got towed and everything."

"What?" Soraya panicked. "Where are you now? Do you need me to pick you up?"

"No, I'm okay. Nate came to get me. I'm at his house, and I'm going to England with him in the morning."

"What? The morning? You leaving me?"

"I need a vacation, so I'm gonna go."

"I heard the hell out of that. You deserve it. I was wondering when you were going to take a vacay. Will I see you before you leave?"

"I'll be over there to pack in a little bit. You going to be home?"

"I'm not sure. You may have to Facetime me."

"Okay. I'll do that. Talk to you later."

"Later."

Nate came into the living room with a smile on his face. "Everything is all worked out. You want some water or something?"

"Yes, please."

"Come into the kitchen with me."

I followed him to the kitchen, feeling like a burden had been lifted off me. Even though my car was gone, it was the last thing I had left to remind me of Avian.

Nate took a bottle of water from the fridge and handed it to me. "Thank you," I said.

"You're welcome."

I unscrewed the top and drank the water. He watched me with his hands resting on the counter behind him. "You look good," he said.

"You say that every time you see me."

"That's because it's true."

"The police officer thought so too," I said with a smile.

"I bet he did."

"That's the reason he didn't give me a speeding ticket."

"He knew what was up," he replied. "Come here."

I put the bottle on the counter, and he took hold of my waist.

"I'm so glad that you're coming with me," he said. "I'm not gonna lie. I thought I was going to lose you."

I threw my lips to his and kissed him deeply. He wrapped his strong arms around me and squeezed. As he guided me to his bedroom, his lips never left mine. We undressed one another passionately. After putting on a condom, I lay back on his bed, waiting for his body to cover mine. As soon as he entered my body, I closed my eyes. He was working with something sweet and thick. My body loved the way he fit. Clenching my walls around him, I moaned.

I bit my lower lip as my nails raked at his back. With each stroke, I reached my peak faster. My juices trickled down the inside of both thighs. I trembled as his pumps became more profound and more laborious. His slow, passionate lovemaking quickly turned into straight-up fucking. His strokes were deeper, harder, and faster.

I moaned. Nate lifted me in his arms and flipped me so that I could lie on top of him. He took hold of my face with both hands and kissed me. I sucked his tongue for a while as I rode him. Our shadows danced against the wall. My orgasm came as I tilted my head back. His hands moved up to my breasts, and Nate was moaning right along with me. The sounds of his pleasure stimulated me even more.

Chapter 38

Kyree

I didn't want to get up from the bed. I didn't want to move at all. I'd lost my girl, and I hadn't seen my son in weeks. I picked up my phone from my end table. It was 8:35 a.m. I had one missed call from Fendi and zero texts. My phone usually had at least five text messages when I woke up every morning. I was hoping one of them would've been from Soraya. When thinking of her, there was an ache that came and went, always returning in quiet moments. This was how the universe decided to tell me that my life was officially fucked up. I wanted so much to talk and laugh like we once did. Her absence was my fault, and I had to own it.

Sighing and feeling sick to my stomach, I clicked on Apple Music to put on a playlist to at least get me out of bed. I found a playlist that was recommended for me, and I hit play. Li'l Baby's "Close Friends" came on, and it made me think of her. Shit, everything I did made me think of her, making the pain all the worse, keeping my feelings too raw.

I got out of bed, showered, and dried off. I dressed in joggers and a hoodie. I went into the kitchen to get a bowl of Crunch Berries cereal and realized that I didn't have any milk. I threw on my shoes, got in my car, and headed to the store. On the drive to the store, I was so close to Soraya's apartment that it made me think of her.

Her beautiful smile flashed in my mind, and it felt like someone was twisting a knife into my heart. I wondered what she was up to.

As I pulled up alongside the curb in front of her apartment, I saw her car parallel parked across the street between two other vehicles. I took a deep breath. I was going to drive myself crazy if I didn't try to explain myself this one last time. Against all sense and sensibility, I was standing at her front door, breathing in and out, thinking about what I was going to say differently to get her to forgive me. I stuck my index finger out to ring the doorbell, but before I could ring it, I heard the locks on the door.

I felt relieved that I didn't have to ring the bell but nervous to see her reaction. I didn't even care if she was about to swing the door open to cuss me out. If she was done with me, I didn't have a choice but to accept that.

The door opened, and her face was just as pretty as the day I first saw her. She had the trash in her hand and wireless earbuds in her ears. As she jumped back at the sight of me, she removed one of her earbuds. "Kyree, what the fuck are you doing here? You scared me."

"I'm sorry. I didn't mean to scare you. I had to see you. You haven't been returning my calls, and you blocked me on Facebook."

She scowled, looking clearly agitated. Immediate dissatisfaction was all over her face. All I wanted to do was feel her in my arms again. I wanted to make things right between us before the aching in my heart killed me.

"Let me take the trash down for you," I volunteered, reaching my hand out to her.

She snatched away, saying, "Nah, I got it." She walked past me and went down the stairs.

I stayed right there, unsure of what to do next. "Fuck," I said under my breath. She was not going to make this easy for me.

After tossing the trash, she jogged back up the stairs and said, "Look, I don't know why you're here, but you gotta go."

"I'll leave, but can we talk first?" I pleaded.

She sighed loudly but opened the door. She let me in with a look of annoyance. I walked inside, and the fruity scent of her body spray was floating through the air. God, I missed her so much. Since she was still standing at the front door, I figured she was only giving me a few minutes to speak my piece.

"I've been thinking about you constantly. You're always on my mind. Since you blocked my calls, I wanted to tell you to your face that I'm sorry I lied about everything. The last thing I wanted to do was hurt you." I reached toward her to hold both of her hands, but she folded her arms across her chest.

"Don't, Kyree."

Staring at her twisted lips and furrowed eyebrows, all I could think about was kissing away the pain I'd caused. I pressed my body up against hers because I needed to breathe her air. To my surprise, she didn't snatch away from me. I could feel her shaky breath as I dropped my head down to snuggle my nose in the crook of her neck, inhaling her scent.

"Soraya," I whispered as I softly placed tiny kisses along her neck. "Please hear me out, baby."

I was making a bold move that would cause her to either slap me or embrace me. The second she closed her eyes, I kissed her tender lips. The soft moan that I heard escape from under her breath gave me hope, but then it came to a screeching halt.

"Kyree, don't," she said in a gentle tone. "Please leave and go back to your wife and son."

"Don't make me leave before you hear me out."

She pulled entirely away and yelled, "I don't want to hear shit from you! You had plenty of time to tell me about your marriage, about her still living in your house, about her being pregnant again. You chose to give half-truths and flat-out lies!"

"Soraya, I'm sorry for everything. I'm married, but I'm not happy in my marriage. I don't love India the way a man should love his wife. I married her because she was pregnant," I said, hoping that would soften her up.

She opened the door to let me out. Soraya wasn't trying to hear the shit I had to say.

Dropping my head, I left her apartment. She quickly locked the door behind me. I trotted down the stairs to get back to my car.

I was going to have to give her more time. I was going to be waiting, and I was going to wait for however long she wanted me to, because I was in love with her. I would come running if she ever needed me. But then my chest ached as reality set in that I had lost her for good. No one could ever replace her, because she was unlike anyone I had ever met.

Chapter 39

Soraya

Right after Kyree popped his ass up on my doorstep like I told him it was cool, I was about to get dressed because Journey was on her way to talk business. I didn't care if Kyree was the one who had linked me up with Journey. I was still going to use her because I liked her work. That was the whole point of networking. I didn't need him to keep that connection linked.

I returned to my bedroom and saw that I had a missed call from Jacoury. I hit him back, but we played phone tag.

His voicemail greeted me, and I said, "Hey, sorry I missed your call. Call me back when you get this."

As soon as I was showered and dressed, the doorbell rang. I answered the door, and a light-skinned woman with curves was standing there holding a black leather portfolio. I shouldn't have been surprised that Journey was so pretty, with her almost-bald blond hair. She was well dressed in a peach sundress and jeweled sandals.

"Journey?" I asked.

"Yeah. Soraya?"

"Yeah. Come on in."

She strutted inside and looked around while I closed the door. "Nice place," she complimented me.

"Thanks. We can sit over here on the couch."

Journey sat, and I sat on the love seat. "I brought my portfolio for you to look at," she said.

"Okay cool. Thanks for meeting me so early. I don't usually get up this early. I want to discuss pricing and dates so we can get started."

"No problem. I'm always up early. I charge one hundred dollars for the first hour, and then it's fifty dollars for each added hour. If you want the photos edited, it's an additional seventy-five. Kyree called me and mentioned that he didn't know if you would still want to do business since you broke up. I'm happy that we could still do business regardless."

"Kyree told you that we broke up?" I fluttered my eyelashes, feeling confused about why he would divulge our business like that.

She noticed my attitude and quickly replied, "Yeah, but he didn't talk shit or nothing. I've known Kyree for years. And I've never seen him care about a woman the way he cares for you."

I took a good look at the way she talked about Kyree. The slight smile on her face told me she and Kyree were more than friends at some point.

"Well, Kyree and I are done, but I don't really like discussing personal things during business." I continued to flip through her portfolio. I loved her work, but if she wanted to get business rolling, we were going to have to stop talking about that no-good, lying snake.

"I understand completely. Before we get down to business, if you don't mind me asking, why'd you break up with him?"

Why didn't he tell her that? I felt confused, and this bitch was nosy as hell. This was none of her business, but since she wanted to take it there, I was going to get it out the way so we could focus on business afterward.

"He's a liar," I replied straightforwardly. "And he's married, which was something he did not tell me. I can't handle all of that."

"You didn't know that he was married in the beginning?"

"No." I changed the subject. "Wow, your work is so dope. I can't wait to see what kind of ideas you have for my label, Paradise You."

"Wait, I'm sorry. How did you find out he was married? Was she the one who told you? You know his wife?"

This bitch was getting on my nerves. Why was any of this critical for her to know? Now I had to know what her deal was. "Have you ever met his wife?" I asked.

Journey nodded with an eye roll. "Yeah, she's dreadful. I hate that bitch. She made my life a living hell. Since I steer clear of her, I don't have any drama in my life."

"Why would she make your life a living hell? Was she jealous of your friendship with Kyree?"

"Well, I don't know if he told you this, but Kyree and I used to be involved. This was before they were married, but I knew they were together. Kyree charmed me, and shit got real ugly. They were expecting their son, Kai. Anyway, she busted the windows out my car, she put sugar in my gas tank, and she ruined a few photo shoots I had lined up. The bitch is crazy, but I'm sure you know that."

"Thankfully, I've never had to deal with her like that. Like I said, I didn't know they were together like that. Kyree didn't tell me that you and him ever were a thing. He just said he knew someone who would be dope to work with."

"We dated six years ago, but it's not like that anymore. He's my friend."

I could see it in her eyes. She still had feelings for him, even with the way he was. She would fuck him again if he let her. I handed her the portfolio. I was done, and my mind was made up. I didn't want to do business with Journey. We weren't about to become BFFs and start talking about who fucked Kyree the best.

"I appreciate you coming by. I'll call you when I get my money together," I lied.

Journey stood up. "Okay, well, let me know a date, and we will get started."

I walked her to the door. It was like she couldn't wait to talk to me about Kyree. Was she making sure I was done with him so she could sink her claws back into him? Whatever her deal was, I didn't want to know shit about it. Journey left, and I locked the door behind her.

My cell phone was ringing, so I ran to my room and picked it up from my bed. It was Jacoury. "Hello," I cooed into the phone.

"Hey, sexy. What you doing?"

"Just wrapped up some business. We playing phone tag this morning."

"Yeah, I was out grocery shopping with your mom. She didn't want to go alone, plus she wanted to see me. I was her chauffeur for the morning."

I wanted to feel jealous that he was spending time with my mama, but then again, I was happy that he was so willing to take my mother shopping. It was cute that they spent a lot of time together. "I'm glad you enjoyed the time with my mom. I haven't talked to her in a few days. I need to see her. Speaking of, I will call her later."

"She mentioned she wanted us to come by and have dinner soon. I adore your mom. She was there for me in some of my darkest times."

I felt guilty for not being down for him the way my mom had. "I'm sorry I wasn't there for you, Jacoury."

"You already apologized. Don't trip, for real. Anyway, can I come over to see your pretty face or what?"

I grinned from ear to ear. "Yeah. Come on. I really need to see you right now."

"Okay. I'm on my way."

I went to the bathroom, relieved my bladder, and washed my hands. I looked at myself in the mirror, checked my hair. I looked good. I went back into the living room and turned on the TV. I checked my DVR to see if *Ambitions* had recorded.

My doorbell rang. I walked toward the front door, feeling excited. When I peeked through the peephole, I sucked my teeth and exhaled because it wasn't Jacoury. It was Kyree. What didn't this fool understand?

I decided not to answer it. Another set of footsteps came up the stairs. Shit, Jacoury was here, and Kyree was still on my doorstep, looking like a fucking idiot.

I flung the door opened, and said, "Hey, babe."

They both looked at me and replied, "Hey."

"Why the fuck you here?" I screamed at Kyree. "Like I told you earlier, go away!"

Kyree glared at me as I pulled Jacoury in by his T-shirt and slammed the door.

"I was about to say, how you going to ask me to come over when you got this nigga here?" Jacoury scowled.

"I wouldn't set you up like that. He's stalking me. He popped up over here earlier, and now he's back. He's freaking me out."

"Where's Kaeja?"

"With Nate. They are going to England for a movie he's shooting." I ran my hands through my hair. My heart was skipping beats because I was scared.

"How long will she be gone?" he asked.

"A few weeks at least. She's taking some much-needed vacation time."

"I don't think you should be here alone. I don't want to have to put my hands on this nigga, so we're going to my house, and that's where you're going to stay until Kaeja comes back."

"Good idea. Let me go grab my things."

Chapter 40

Kyree

So this was why she wasn't trying to see me anymore. I saw the nigga with India's friend, Tiffany, at the House of Blues on the first night I met Soraya. I was no longer confused about how she knew about my marriage. He had to be the one who told her. When I saw his tall, lanky ass come up those stairs, I felt instant rage. Hearing Soraya call him babe instead of me rocked me to my core.

I drove away from her complex with my emotions spiraling out of control, but I didn't go far. I parked a few blocks up, behind a few other cars. I was waiting for him to leave, but they came out of her apartment with her suitcase. He kissed her before she got into her car. He got into his Jeep, pulled away, and she followed him.

She was out of fucking bounds, and all I was trying to do was make it right between us. I thought about all the kinky, freaky shit she did with me, and it had me wondering if she did the same shit with him.

I waited before I followed them. I needed to see what was going on. Judging by the suitcase, she wasn't going to be home for a few days. I felt like a damn fool after following them to his house. He pulled into the driveway, and she pulled up behind him. I parked down the street. I watched them get out of their cars and walk to his front door hand in hand. I felt queasy, like I was going to throw up. They say that pain goes away with time and in time things will get better, but how could things get better when I didn't want the reason for my pain to be forgotten? If getting past the pain meant letting her go, then I chose to suffer for the rest of my life.

So many times, I wanted to run to the door and demand to talk to her, but I talked myself out of it. It wasn't even twenty minutes before Soraya came out of the house alone. She got into her car, backed out of the driveway, and headed down the opposite end of the street. I followed her until she stopped at Whole Foods.

Luckily for me, she didn't notice. I parked on the other end of the parking lot. I entered the other side of the store. I grabbed a handbasket and passed each aisle, looking for her. I didn't have to find her. She saw me. To my surprise, she marched toward me, pushing that cart fast.

"What the fuck is your problem, Kyree? What are you doing here? And don't say your ass was doing some shopping, because this ain't Watts."

I didn't know how to respond to her talking to me with authority like that, as if she hated me. I had to look around to remind myself that this was a public place, so I kept my voice down.

"Soraya, if you hadn't blocked me from calling, I wouldn't be acting like a madman. I don't usually do shit like this, but I got this shit bad, and I don't know what to do about it. I love you so much. I can't get you out of my head."

"So you think by following me like a crazy psycho that would make me want to talk to you? Are you dumb? We don't have anything to discuss. Step the fuck off and stay away from me or else I'm calling the police."

"The police? Really? Look, if you're done with me, just say it. I don't have a choice but to accept that."

She looked at me and replied, "I already told your deaf ass that we're through. Why are you stalking me, Kyree?"

"Man, ain't nobody stalking you. I want to talk. That's it."

"Well, I hope you got your listening ears on right now. We're done, Kyree. I'm back with my first love."

"Your first love? Ain't that Tiffany's nigga who just got out of prison?"

"He's not with her, but you don't need to be worried about him." She looked around the store to see if anyone else had heard us arguing in the middle of the aisle. "Look, don't come near me anymore. I mean that shit. Goodbye, Kyree."

She walked away and left the cart right there without getting anything she came to the store for. I didn't chase after her. Her words stung as they rang in my ears. I walked to the dairy section of the store, grabbed a half gallon of milk, and checked out.

Chapter 41

Kaeja

For the first time in my life, I was preparing to leave the United States. I was stepping outside of my comfort zone and going to a whole new country. Nate and I walked through first-class security after our luggage was checked. No line. No waiting. No stress. Thanks to him, I got to experience my first international first-class flight. I was feeling like royalty as we walked into the plush departure lounge for first-class passengers. They were serving complimentary food and drinks while the passengers waited for the flight to board.

"This is nice," I said.

"Yeah. This is the only way I like to fly. You want something to drink?" he asked.

"I want some water."

"Let me get that for you."

Right before he could get it, they announced our flight was boarding for first class.

"You'll get it once we are on the plane," he said.

We walked to the boarding area. He allowed me to walk through first. I showed the flight attendant my boarding pass, and I walked down the corridor to the plane. He was right behind me. The first-class cabin was spacious, and it was big enough for both of us. Our seats were also a flatbed with personal pillows and blankets. We even had a private TV and a window.

He smiled. "This your first time flying international?"

"Yes."

"I'm glad you are experiencing something for the first time with me."

"Me too. Can I sit near the window?"

"Sure."

I took the seat near the window, and he sat next to me.

The stewardess came to us. "Hello. Would you two like anything to drink?"

"Yes, can I have water with a few lemon slices?" I said.

"And I'll have a vodka tonic with lime, please," Nate replied.

"Sure thing. I'll be right back."

"I've clearly been missing out," I said. "I flew first class with my parents years ago, but I don't remember it being anything like this."

"Flights that go overseas are a lot different from the standard business class."

"I see. Thank you, Nate, for inviting me."

"I'm happy you're with me."

The stewardess was back. Nate got his vodka, and I had my water. I got comfortable to prepare myself for takeoff. I rested my head on Nate's shoulder as he sipped his vodka while others filed onto the plane.

"This is what it's like to roll with a movie star, huh?"

"Yes, indeed. It's something to get used to."

"Oh, I definitely can get used to this."

Nate put his free hand in mine. "Good."

"Do you ever have to deal with paparazzi?"

"Yes and no. Most celebs call paparazzi on themselves, to be honest. I'm a low-key actor, and I'm not on the A-list, so nobody is really checking for me like that."

"Are there any other celebs in this movie?"

"You may recognize a few. I won't drop names, but once you're on set, you'll see."

"The suspense is killing me."

He chuckled. "Okay, I'll drop a hint. One of them is an Oscar-winning actor. He's African American. He is undisputedly one of the best actors alive, and he's also directing this film. Most women would say he's handsome."

"Denzel Washington?"

"Hey, you're pretty good at this."

I sat up and looked into his eyes. "Seriously? Denzel Washington?"

He nodded as if it were no big deal. "Yeah."

My hand covered my chest, and my eyes were wide. "Will I have a chance to meet him?"

"Your chances are pretty high, beautiful."

"Oh, my God. I can't believe this. Anyone else I need to prepare myself for?"

He chuckled. "I'm sure, but the rest is a surprise."

Being around Avian, I'd met various levels of celebrities, so I knew how to act around them, but I had never been in the presence of an A-lister before. I didn't know how Nate could be so calm about any of this.

"Wow. What are the plans day one?"

"Well, I won't have to be on set until a few hours after my arrival. We should settle into the suite and just wing it."

"Sounds good to me." I rested my head back on his shoulder. He kissed the top of my head.

Chapter 42

Soraya

I couldn't do any grocery shopping at Whole Foods because I didn't want to talk to Kyree anymore. I wound up going to Ralph's on West Ninth, which was only a block away. I looked in my rearview mirror the entire time to see if I was being followed. Thankfully, Kyree did not follow me, and I was able to shop for things I needed for my stay at Jacoury's. As I pulled up behind Jacoury's Jeep, he came out of the house to help me bring the groceries in.

He took one look at my face and asked, "What's the matter?"

"Nothing," I replied, taking two bags up the walkway to his door. I walked inside the house and placed them on his kitchen island. He set the last two bags next to them.

"Something's up. Talk to me," he said.

"Kyree was at the grocery store when I got there, but I handled it."

"What?" He grimaced. "What you mean he was at the store?"

"I'm not sure if he followed me or whatnot, but he was there. I told him that if he doesn't stop this shit, then I'm calling the police."

"Fuck the police, Buttercup. I'll fuck his ass up, period."

"Hopefully it won't have to come to that."

"But if it does, I'm ready for whatever."

"I know."

He helped me put the groceries away. I went to my suitcase, unzipped it, and realized I'd left my laptop at home. "Shit," I said.

"What?"

"I forgot my laptop at home. I need it. I was working on a few designs."

"Well, let's go get it. You drive. I ride."

"Okay."

I grabbed my purse, and we walked out of the house.

We walked up my steps, but I halted once I reached the top.

Jacoury said, "What the fuck?"

The door had a huge dent the size of a shoe near the bottom of the door, and it was slightly open. Splinters on the doorframe were sticking out. Someone had kicked in the door. I backed up toward the steps, afraid that whoever did that was still inside.

Jacoury pushed it open slowly.

"Don't go in there," I said, feeling scared. "I'm calling the police."

I grabbed his hand, and we walked down the stairs. I didn't stop until we got to the curb. I dialed 911.

"911, state your emergency please."

"Yes, my apartment has been broken into."

"What is your address?"

"Thirty-one fifty-five Wilshire."

"Are you at the residence now?"

"I am standing outside."

"Is the intruder there?"

"I'm not sure. I didn't go inside. The door is kicked in."

"Okay. Do not go inside. I'll send an officer your way now."

"Thank you."

I ended the call, shaking my head. If Kyree had done this, I was going to lose my mind. I scanned the street to see if I could see his car, but I didn't see it.

Jacoury kept his eyes on the stairs to my apartment as he rubbed his chin. "This nigga lost his mind."

"You think he did it too?"

"Of course he did. Weak-ass, salty-ass nigga. I'm telling you right now, I'm beating his ass on sight."

"And then you'll be back in jail. Let the police do what they need to do."

Jacoury was silent, and we stayed quiet until the police pulled up fifteen minutes later. Two officers stepped outside of their car, one black male and a white female. The female officer asked, "What's going on here?"

"Someone kicked in my door. We didn't go inside, but we just need a safety check."

The black officer said, "We'll check it out for you. Which apartment?"

"Two twelve. Right up those stairs right there." I pointed.

"Got it. Stay right here."

"Okay," I replied.

Jacoury and I watched the officers walk up the stairs and disappear inside of the apartment. Jacoury said, "It may be time for y'all to move."

"And where do you suggest we move to?"

"Somewhere safe."

"Ma'am," the white officer called, "nobody's inside, but they trashed the place. You want to come see if anything is missing?"

I walked toward the apartment with Jacoury following. When we got inside the apartment, my mouth dropped open. The word "Bitch" was spray-painted in red on the living room wall. The couch was ripped, and the filling was spilling out. The TV was shattered, lying on the ground faceup. The bookshelf was thrown down. My laptop was snapped in half and thrown on the floor. I ran to my bedroom, but nothing was touched in there. I went to Kaeja's room, and it was still intact. Instant tears fell.

"Is anything missing?" the black officer asked.

"No, just damaged items."

"The fuck, man?" Jacoury scowled. "This is some straight bullshit."

"Ma'am, do you know anyone who would want to do this? If nothing is missing, this could be a personal attack."

"Well, this guy I used to mess with has been harassing me today. He showed up here unannounced earlier, then he followed me to the grocery store. I told him to fuck off. Then I come home to this."

The white officer put on some gloves and said, "We're going to dust the place for fingerprints. Try not to touch anything. We should be able to match the prints. My partner here will get a statement and list the damaged items."

I nodded. While I listed off the things that were broken, she interrupted us.

"Look," she said, picking up a note from the kitchen table. "I found a note." She read it aloud, "'Bitch, stay away from my husband. You've been warned.'"

The black officer said, "Wow. She must be crazy to leave that. Do you know this person?"

"India," I replied, feeling confused. Why was she bothering me? I wasn't with Kyree.

"Do you have an address for India?" the female officer asked. "What's her last name?"

"Kirk. I'm not sure where she lives."

"She lives with her mother off Rosecrans," Jacoury said.

"We'll look her up to see if we can get an address. We're going to keep dusting for prints."

"It will probably be a good thing to get a house alarm or something to prevent this from happening again. Do you want to press charges?" the black officer asked.

"Yes."

"All right," he replied.

We wrapped up my statement, and they left after dusting for prints. It was left up to us to clean this place up.

"I can't believe this," I said. "Kyree's crazy wife is just as nuts as he is."

"India ain't wrapped too tight."

"This must've been what Journey meant."

"Who's Journey?"

"Someone who used to fuck with Kyree. I was going to work with her on some photos for Paradise You. I'm emotionally spent. I gotta get a new laptop to work. I don't know if my hard drive can be saved. Look, we'll get it cleaned up tomorrow and get an alarm system."

"Fuck that. You need to move," Jacoury said. "Soraya, I don't feel comfortable with knowing that her crazy ass is trying to come for you over a nigga who don't want her and you don't want him. Not to mention, while he's busy trying to follow you, she's following him."

I agreed. "You mind if I stay with you until we figure this out?"

"You can stay as long as you need."

"Let me see if this door will at least close. I may have to call maintenance to get a new door." I closed it, but it wouldn't lock. "I'm going to leave a message since the office is closed and see if they can replace it."

"Good idea."

I tried to reach Kaeja to let her know what happened, but her phone was doing something weird. It would ring, but then it would disconnect. I figured it was because she was still on the plane. She did say it would take ten hours nonstop, so she wouldn't get there until the following morning.

Jacoury was chilling, watching *SportsCenter*. March Madness was approaching.

My phone rang while I was pulling up Skype to call Kaeja. An unknown Los Angeles number was calling. "Hello?" I answered.

"Hello. Is this Soraya? This is Officer Tate from the LAPD."

"Yes, this is she."

"I'm following up on your break-in. India Kirk was arrested this morning."

"Thank you for the update."

"You're welcome. You are still pressing charges, right?"

"Yes, of course."

"Okay. You enjoy the rest of your evening."

"Thank you." I ended the call.

"Who was that?" Jacoury asked.

"LAPD. They arrested Kyree's wife."

"Good. Serves her ass right for doing that shit! Bet she thinks twice before doing that to anyone else."

"Crazy bitch," I replied.

Chapter 43

Kyree

I flipped through the channels to see if any good movies were playing. I was beating myself up mentally. I was trying to swallow the hard pill of rejection. While I calmed my thoughts, India's mom called me to my surprise.

"Hello?" I asked, answering my phone.

"Kyree, you need to pick up your son. India's dumb ass done got arrested for fucking with that girl you were messing with."

"What? When?"

"Just now. The police came and got her."

"What did she do?" I asked, feeling instantly upset.

"Kicked the girl's door in and messed her place up. I don't know why she does this without thinking about Kai. I gotta work, so I can't watch him."

"Don't worry, Sheila. I'm on my way."

I ended the call and rushed to pick up my son.

No matter how busy I kept myself, I hadn't stopped thinking about Soraya for two days. I was sure she hated me, especially after what India had done to her place. Her beauty was a painting that I felt were for my eyes only. I wanted to be with her so I could catch a whiff of her sweet scent. She was drowning me in my dreams, and

I woke up hating that my dreams weren't real. I was her lover, and she was mine. I wanted to marry her, make love to her, have kids with her. I was torturing myself, but I didn't know how to turn the shit off. How could I end this vortex, this flooding, this profoundly buried love, its blaze in my heart that burned only for her? Because of her absence, the pain had a grip on my heart. I was having a tough time coping.

While India was in jail, I wasted no time filing for full custody. My son needed to be with me if she wanted to act like this. Since she was in custody, the judge granted an emergency hearing and gave me temporary full custody until we could do mediation.

After I picked up Kai from school, we went home. India was sitting on my porch, waiting for me. I didn't know she had been released.

Kai got out of the car and ran to her. She showered his face with kisses. "Mommy missed you so much. Look at you. I feel like you grew so much in just two days. I love you."

"I love you too, Mom," Kai said with the biggest smile on his face.

She looked up at me and said, "Hey. Thanks for keeping him."

"No need to thank me. I'm his father."

"You mind if we talk?"

I walked up to the door and unlocked it. "Kai, go to your room for a minute."

Kai nodded and skipped to his room.

"What's up?" I asked.

"You tryin' to take my son from me?"

"What the fuck do you expect?" I replied. "You made me lose the one woman I love, and you want to question me?"

"I made you lose that bitch? You're blaming me when you're the one who lied to her from the jump?"

"Yes, you! If it weren't for you, I would've been able to get her back. You had to follow me over there and fuck with her." I glared at her.

"You fucked that up before I got to the bitch. I didn't know you two were over, so that was my fault for assuming she was still dealing with your dumb ass."

"Whatever. I don't want to talk about it. Back to what you were saying, yes, I want full custody of my son."

"You're a worthless son of a bitch! I did two days in the county jail, thinking about how I was going to pull this family back together. Yeah, I fucked with your bitch, and I paid the price for it, too. You ain't getting Kai."

"You clearly didn't read the ex parte hearing papers, did you? Kai is staying with me until we go to mediation. You take him from here and you'll be right back in jail. Try me."

She had tears in her eyes as she said, "Damn, you're an asshole! Why are you doing this to me?" She tried to touch my arm. "Please, don't do this."

My lips curled into a snarl. "India, I swear you better not touch me."

"Or what? Are you going to hit me again, you bitch-ass nigga?" She grabbed my face with both hands and tried to force me to kiss her.

"Damn it, India! Get the fuck off me!"

"No!" she yelled and gripped me harder as tears fell from her eyes. "I won't let you go because I love you, and that bitch ain't thinking about you. She's with Jacoury. You need to forget about your precious Soraya and spend the rest of your life with me. Ain't nobody gonna put up with ya shit like me. I'm your wife. We are a family."

"India, stop!" I shoved her so hard she tumbled to the floor.

She sobbed, "I really don't mean shit to you, do I?"

I walked to the door and opened it. "Get out, India."

Instead of walking out the door, she rushed to Kai's room. "You want to come with Mommy?"

"India, don't—"

"Yeah," Kai replied.

"Come on." She wiped her tears and took his hand, and they walked toward me at the door.

"India, stop!"

She rolled her eyes and kept on walking out the door.

"Fuck," I said under my breath.

I wasn't going to act a fool with Kai right there. All I could do was close the door and sit on the couch with my hands over my face. My son wanted to go with her, so what was I supposed to do? I couldn't understand why India's crazy ass had to really act so stupid all the time. This shit with her was never-ending.

My cell was vibrating on the coffee table. Fendi was hitting me up. I'd sent him a text earlier to see if he wanted to hang out. It had been months since we'd seen each other.

I answered, "What up?"

"Gucc, where you at?"

"I'm at the crib. Nigga, where you been?"

"Man, I been traveling with these bitches, feel me? I'm back in town, though. Ay, you got li'l man with you?"

"Not right now I don't. Nigga, come through so we can get a drink or something. A nigga needs that for real."

Fendi replied, "I'm pulling up to your crib right now. Open the door."

I got up from the couch and unlocked the door. "It's open."

"A'ight. I'll be in." He ended the call.

I sat on the couch, and Fendi walked in. He closed and locked the door behind him. He flopped down on the love seat and took a small bag of coke out of his pocket.

"Really?" I asked, giving him a hard look.

"Hey, you may not fuck with the shit no mo', but I do."
He put in on the coffee table and started cutting it with
his driver's license to form a line. "Gucc, you know that
nigga Jacoury?"

"Yeah, he's fucking with Soraya now."

"Right, and he used to fuck with Tiff."

"And?"

"I was over there, right, and she started telling me
how much shit this nigga Jacoury was talking about you.
She said he couldn't stop venting about how you were
dogging Soraya."

"Hold up. What?"

Fendi hit two lines of powder and sniffed. "Yeah. While
he was locked up, Tiff held him down. You need to holler
at the nigga, because if he didn't open his fucking mouth
about India, you and Soraya would still be together."

I wasn't going to pretend that what he told me wasn't
fucking with me. I was going to have to holler at Jacoury.
"Let me hit that shit," I said.

"Go 'head," Fendi replied.

I cut a few lines and snorted them. As soon as the drip
happened down the back of my throat, that shit hit me.
Fendi had some pure shit, and I was on quick. "Damn," I
said.

"Yeah, that shit's pure. Go easy. So, Gucc, you gon'
holler at the nigga?"

"Yeah, I'll holler at him."

"If he doesn't do nothin' else, he needs to respect ya
name. I ain't never seen you walk the straight and narrow
until you met Soraya. That nigga played dirty and took ya
bitch!"

Jacoury took my bitch. The thought had me hopping
up from that couch and going into my closet for my gun.
My brain told me to go over to Jacoury's house since I
knew where he lived.

"Gucc, where you going?" Fendi asked. "You hollering at him now?"

"Yeah, you rolling?"

"Nigga, let's go."

We walked out of the house. I locked the door and got into my car. I started up the car, and Fendi was extra chatty. Coke did that to him. He was rambling on about how this new chick tried to play him. I tuned him out, all while thinking about what I was going to say to this bitch-ass nigga.

The drive to Jacoury's side of Los Angeles took about forty-five minutes because of traffic, so we kept hitting the pack to maintain the high. That cocaine had my heart hammering, and my mind kept flickering to the gun I had in my pocket. What was I going to say to this nigga? I felt like I could drown in air, suffocate from holding my breath too long, so I released it from my mouth. I was too high, and I didn't have liquor to balance out the zoom.

Fendi turned on some music and turned it up loud. The closer I got to Jacoury's house, the louder the music seemed to grow. My heart rate quickly surpassed the hard-hitting "808" coming through my speakers. As I pulled up, it felt like my heart had stopped entirely, and my stomach dropped to the ground.

Chapter 44

Soraya

Jacoury and I were snuggled up watching TV. I didn't mind watching ESPN with him because it reminded me of our college days. Falling back in love with him was the natural part. Admitting my feelings for him was hard, but I was glad we were back together. Every time he looked at me, it was as if every ounce of my breath was taken from me. Every time he kissed me, it felt like the world could stop just for us. Every time he held my face between his hands, it felt like he had untied all these knots I'd created.

He traced my lips lightly with the tip of his finger. I gazed into his eyes intently.

"Buttercup?"

"Yes, Jacoury."

"Marry me."

"What you say?"

"Marry me."

"Ooooh, you're so romantic. If you had a ring, I probably would say yes."

"That's all it takes? A ring?"

"That's how a man is supposed to propose, isn't it?"

"Everyone has their own style. I ain't everybody."

"Well, I would want a ring. No ring, no marriage. Period."

"I thought you'd say that." He got up and disappeared inside his bedroom. He came out of the bedroom with his hands behind his back. "The other day when I told you I was out with your mom grocery shopping, I was actually shopping for a ring. I needed her approval. So, uh, what were you saying about a ring?"

"Jacoury! What? Let me see it!" I squealed.

He pulled the ring box from behind his back and opened it. He revealed a gorgeous, flawless teardrop diamond ring.

"I want you to be my—"

"Yes!" I hollered.

He took the ring out and put it on my finger. It fit perfectly.

"I ain't big on words and shit. Your mother said you would love it."

"She knows my style. I'm surprised she didn't ruin the surprise. She usually cannot keep a secret."

"I told her that if she kept it to herself, I would pay for a trip to Hawaii."

I laughed. "You bribed my mama?"

He laughed with me. "I had to. I love you."

"I love you more."

He softly kissed me, and I melted into his arms. It took a man in Gucci to help me realize that my one true love had been in my face all along. With Jacoury, our love felt true. True love felt like life was beautiful.

"I'm hungry. Let's go get something to eat," he said. "Let's get some tacos."

"Okay," I replied. "Ernesto's?"

"You read my mind, babe. I swear. I'll drive, so pull your car out and park on the curb."

"Okay."

He grabbed his keys, and we walked out of the house. He hit the unlock button on his car. I pulled my car out of the driveway and parked near the curb in front of his house. Right before we could get into his car, I saw Kyree's car pulling up. My stomach started hurting. I thought after two days he would be done.

The passenger window rolled down, and Fendi was sitting there with a mean mug on his face. Kyree leaned over and said in a rush, "Come here, Soraya. Let me talk to you. Baby, listen, let me talk to you."

Jacoury said, "Niggaaaaa, if you don't get the fuck off my property with that shit."

Kyree hopped out of the car. He had a gun in his right hand, dangling at his side. "I'm about sick of ya mouth, nigga. Now, what's all this shit I'm hearing? You speaking on me? Keep my muthafuckin' name out ya mouth, punk-ass nigga."

I shrieked, backing up. My instinct told me to run into the house, but Jacoury walked toward Kyree, ready for a fight. The gun didn't faze him one bit. The streets taught him to fear no man, only God.

"What the fuck you gon' do with that? You want to talk to me like a man, or you want to shoot me over someone who don't belong to you? Put the gun down, bitch, so we can fade like real men." They were face-to-face then. If hatred were visible, the air would've been red as blood.

Kyree smirked, rubbed his nose, and sniffled. "Fuck you! She don't belong to you!"

Looking at Kyree, I realized I had never seen him like this. He was starting to sweat, and he kept sniffling as if he had a runny nose. Was he high?

"Check this out. You see that ring on her finger right now? You trippin', comin' to my house lookin' crazy as fuck."

Kyree stepped back and aimed the gun at Jacoury. Jacoury instantly shoved the gun out his face, and they started tussling over it.

I pulled my phone out my purse and dialed 911.

"911, state your emergency."

"I need someone to get over here now! My ex has a gun." Jacoury and Kyree were fighting, struggling over the gun. Every blow had so much force.

Fendi yelled from the car, "Whoop his ass, nigga!"

Kyree was struggling to do so because Jacoury was trying to smash Kyree into the earth. Two blows sent Kyree's head into the concrete.

"Stop fighting!" I hollered. Turning my back to them, I said into the phone, "Lady, look, ping the fucking address! Get here before one of them gets hurt!"

Fendi hopped out of the car to jump on Jacoury.

Bang! Bang! Bang!

Three gunshots cracked as loud as thunder.

I dropped the phone, and when I turned around, Jacoury was falling to the ground.

I screamed.

Kyree's chest was heaving up and down as he stared at me.

Fendi was shouting, "Gucc, let's go! She called the cops, nigga!"

Kyree ran to the car. After Fendi hopped in, he sped away, tires screeching.

I ran to Jacoury with instant tears blurring my vision. "Jacoury! Nooooooo!"

He was bleeding through his chest. Falling to my knees, I put his head in my lap, and placed my hands on his wound to try to stop the bleeding.

"Jacoury, don't you die on me! Don't!" I sobbed as his blood gushed through my hands.

He was gasping for air, and I could hear the blood gurgling in the back of his throat. He started choking.

"Help! Somebody!"

In the distance, an ambulance siren wailed like a baby in distress, the kind of noise that made me sick to my stomach. Jacoury's neighbors came outside, staring, but didn't come toward us. The look on some of their white faces as if this were another gang member shot down by an enemy rocked my core. With each growing second, I feared Jacoury was going to die.

He was trying to talk, but I couldn't make out what he was trying to say.

"Baby, I'm here. I'm here." I rocked his head in my arms.

I could no longer hear the ambulance coming because the sound of my breathing along with Jacoury's had drowned it out. There was a blurred shape through my puffy, crying eyes. Life was leaving my man's eyes. He was turning pale.

A pair of strong hands pulled me up from him as I watched his body be put on a stretcher. They were getting his vital signs.

"He's not going to make it," I heard one of them say. "We have to get him airlifted now."

"Miss, what happened here?" another asked me.

"He was shot." I paused to cry.

"Who shot him?"

"They were fighting, and he had a gun."

"We'll get the police to talk to you when we get to the hospital. We're going to get him airlifted to the hospital."

Waiting for the helicopter to come was more terrifying than seeing him get shot. Every second made my anxiety peak higher. Seeing him on the stretcher with them working on him had me so afraid that he would die. They were trying everything they could to help him. Once the helicopter blew in with a gust of strong wind, they rushed him onto it. I didn't care how they saved him. I just needed him to survive.

I called Ann, Jacoury's mom, and my mommy on my way to the hospital. As soon as I got there, my mother and Ann were walking in behind me. Ann took one look at my bloody clothes and sobbed loudly, "Where's my son?"

"They airlifted him here, so I don't know. We have to check with someone."

My mom wrapped her arms around my shoulder as I cried. "Just pray, baby," she said. "Trust God at this moment. Jacoury will pull through."

Ann asked the receptionist, "Where's my son? His name is Jacoury Morrant, and he was shot."

The receptionist looked up his name. "He's here, but he's in surgery. Go up to the second floor and wait in that lobby. Someone will be out to update you."

We walked to the elevator and went up to the second floor. Silence covered us. Tears fell from our eyes. In the lobby on the second floor, the walls were green, reminded me of spring. There were a few people scattered, waiting to hear about their loved ones.

"What happened, Soraya?" Jacoury's mom questioned.

"I used to see this guy, but I ended it. He's been acting crazy lately. His wife broke into my house, so I've been staying at Jacoury's for the last two days. Jacoury had just proposed, and we were going to get something to eat. Out of nowhere, dude shows up. He and Jacoury got into it. Kyree shot Jacoury."

My mother groaned and reached for my shaking hands.

I continued, "I heard three shots. I am so sorry, Miss Ann. I didn't know this would happen."

She glared at me. I'd never seen her look at me that way. She didn't say that she blamed me for this. She didn't need to. I saw it in the way she looked at me.

I was a wreck. I couldn't stop crying, not even when the police questioned me. I gave them Kyree's name and his address. He was going to pay for this shit. The police had what they needed from me and left.

I cried silently, and my mother held me. I tried to keep my mind still, but it wasn't working. Nothing was working for any of us. Ann paced back and forth, looking at each doctor who came out, hoping he or she would know what was going on. Jacoury's bloodstains on my clothes made me replay in my head what had happened. I feared Kyree. I wanted nothing to do with him ever again. I went into the bathroom to wash my hands.

When I came out of the bathroom, a doctor with the posture of an old Army vet walked to us. She smiled coldly and distantly, trying her best to remain professional. Her face was bare without makeup, and her hair hung loosely at her shoulders.

"Are you the family of Jacoury Morrant?" she asked.

"Yes," Ann replied. "I'm his mother. This is his fiancée and her mother. How is he?"

"Jacoury was shot twice in the chest. The bullets barely missed his heart. He flatlined a few times, but he's stable now. We removed the bullets, and he's out of surgery. The medication has him sleeping. We expect him to wake up within the next hour or two. We do not want him to slip into a coma, so we are keeping an eye on him. If you have any questions for me, please let me know."

"Thank you, Doctor," Ann said. "Can we see him?"

"He's in ICU, so only one in at a time."

"Go ahead, Ann," my mom said. "We'll wait." Ann followed the doctor.

My tears wouldn't stop flowing.

"It's going to be okay, Raya," Mom said. "We love Jacoury, and he made me so happy when he took me to shop for your ring. It looks even more beautiful on your hand."

"What if he dies?" I sobbed. "It's all my fault."

"Shhhh, don't talk like that, Raya. Breathe. Relax. You can go see him in a bit."

I heard loud sobbing in the hallway. I looked up to see Ann wailing. My chest heaved up and down as fear filled me.

My mother and I walked over to her. "Miss Ann?" I asked, reaching out to touch her. I placed my hand on her back and rubbed.

She replied, "I can't see him looking like that! This is too much."

My mother said, "Ann, come sit down. Let's get you some water." Taking Ann's arm, my mother guided her back to the lobby to have a seat.

I drew in a deep breath and exhaled. I wanted to see him, but I wasn't sure which room Ann had come out of.

A nurse came toward me. "Excuse me, can you show me to the ICU?" I asked.

"Sure, what's the patient's name?"

"Jacoury Morrant."

"Follow me."

I followed the nurse down the hall and around a corner. She looked at his name on the board and directed me to his room. Walking in, I wasn't prepared enough to see him in the bed with all those tubes everywhere. All the air felt like it was knocked out of my body at the sight of him. Miss Ann had every reason to react the way she had.

With my heart beating through my stomach, I picked up his hand and held it. I leaned over him and placed a kiss on the side of his face. I cried into his chest. I let it all flow out. All my pain, all my guilt, everything.

"Jacoury, if you can hear me, it's me, Buttercup. I love you so much. I'm sorry about what happened. Today was supposed to be special. You asked me to be your wife, and I pray that when you wake up that you'll still want to be my husband. Lord, if you hear me, please don't take him away from me. I finally figured out what I wanted, and now this? I don't want to live my life without him."

I sobbed, hoping Jacoury wouldn't slip so far away that he would never return.

Jacoury squeezed my hand.

My eyes popped open, and I looked down to see him looking at me. I cried yet laughed as I kissed his lips. My tears wouldn't stop flowing.

Chapter 45

Kyree

"Why the fuck you shoot him?" Fendi asked, snorting coke from the back of his hand.

My heart was racing. A lump was in my throat and wouldn't go away no matter how much I tried to swallow, and my palms were sweaty. I'd never shot anyone before, and I was terrified. I didn't respond to Fendi because I was too busy replaying in my head what had happened.

"Why did he have to challenge me like that?" I thought I'd asked myself that question silently, but it came out instead.

"Jacoury ain't no punk, but neither are you. Damn it, nigga. I thought you were bringing the gun just to scare him."

I weaved in and out of traffic dangerously. Sweat was pouring from my head, and I was half blinded by the glare of headlights. The only thing I was thinking about was getting home to figure out my next move. A car honked at me as I swerved around it.

"Slow down," Fendi complained.

I ignored him and skidded wildly around a corner. My tires squealed as I pushed my engine to the limit. I sped over one hundred miles per hour through red lights. A police car's sirens blared, made a U-turn, and were on my ass.

"Fuck," I said.

"I told your ass to slow down. You bet' not stop now! You got blood on you, a gun on you, and I got the blow on me! Nigga, we're going to jail!"

"Shut the fuck up! If you didn't pump me up to do this shit, I never would've gone over there in the first place. I'm high as fuck. I should've never hit that shit."

"Don't blame the coke, nigga. I told you to talk to him, not kill him."

"You don't know if I killed him."

"I'm pretty sure you did."

I hoped I didn't kill him. I kept racing in the streets to see if I could shake the officer. My heart was beating frantically. I looked in the rearview, and there were now two police cars. My heart was beating so hard that I could feel it in my throat. I was scared that I was going to crash into someone and kill them.

My son's face flashed in my head. What the fuck was I doing? I wanted my son, and I tried to hit the rewind button in my mind to undo what I had just done. This wasn't some nightmare I could wake up from. I took my foot off the gas, and the car started to slow down.

"What the fuck are you doing?" Fendi asked, looking at me as if I'd lost my mind. "You stop this car, the police will either kill us, or we're going to jail."

Without words, I hit the brakes and pulled over. As soon as the car had come to a stop, I put it into park. Fendi hopped out of the car and took off running. I put my hands in the air and waited for the police to approach me.

"Hands up! Hands up! Step out of the car!" they shouted. "Now!"

I opened the door, put my hands up, and got out of the car. I was immediately slammed to the asphalt. Handcuffs were slapped on my wrists.

"Why were you speeding?" one asked.

"You got anything on you that I should be aware of?" another questioned.

I didn't say a word as an officer searched my body. "Got a gun on him."

I'd fucked up. I was going to have to pay for what I'd done. Tears spilled from my eyes onto the asphalt. Within seconds, the cop had my wallet.

"What's your name?" he asked sternly.

I didn't respond.

He read, "'Kyree Kirk.' Didn't we get a call on this one a moment ago?"

Another officer replied, "Let me check."

I breathed in and out, thinking about Soraya telling the police my name because I shot her little boyfriend. I was done. At that moment, the sure knowledge that my son's life would have to go on without me set in.

"That shooting that just happened downtown? A witness said he's the one who shot him."

"You think this is the gun right here?"

"Probably."

"Kyree, did you use this gun to shoot someone tonight?" the same officer who searched me asked.

Again, I didn't respond.

"You have the right to remain silent," he said, reading me my Miranda rights.

I was picked up from the ground and escorted to the police car. The same officer opened the door.

The night seemed to have disappeared as soon as I was inside. Everything was black inside: the seats, the floor, the metal bars between me and the front seat. The officer called in a status report, showing no sympathy for me. As I stared out the window, wondering how I was going to get myself out of this, Fendi was placed in the car behind me.

The End